derailed

About the Author

Jon Ripslinger is a retired English teacher who has been married for fifty years. He is the father of six children and grandfather to twelve children—eleven of them girls—as well as a great-grand-daughter. He is also a Korean War veteran, having served aboard the battleship *USS New Jersey*. After four years in the Navy, he earned a BA degree and a Master degree and taught English in public school systems for thirty-five years, the last thirty-three years at Davenport West High School, Davenport, Iowa. He enjoys fishing, hunting, camping, and hanging out with his kids.

derailed

Jon Ripslinger

flux™

Woodbury, Minnesota

First Edition
First Printing, 2006

Book design by Steffani Chambers
Cover design by Ellen Dahl
Cover image of football © Getty Images
Cover image of rail yard © 2005 Paul Katz / Getty Images
Editing by Rhiannon Ross

Flux, an imprint of Llewellyn Publications

Library of Congress Cataloging-in-Publication Data (pending)
ISBN-13: 978-0-7387-0888-1
ISBN-10: 0-7387-0888-7

Flux
A Division of Llewellyn Worldwide, Ltd.
2143 Wooddale Drive, Dept. 0-7387-0888-7
Woodbury, MN 55125-2989, U.S.A.
www.fluxnow.com

Printed in the United States of America

Acknowledgments

Robert Brown and Sharene Martin of the Wylie-Merrick Literary Agency: Without your guidance this book never would have been published.

Jennifer Ripslinger: Your computer help has been invaluable and is greatly appreciated.

Andrew Karre, Steffani Chambers, Ellen Dahl, and Rhiannon Ross: members of the Flux publishing team who have made the production of this book a great experience for me.

Lastly, this book is dedicated to my wife of fifty years, Mary Colette Shannon Ripslinger, who has always supported my projects. Thank you. And love.

—Jon Ripslinger

one

Monday morning at school, after we won our third football game in a row, ass-kicking convincingly, I might add, Coach Maddox yanked me into his office in the boys' locker room.

It was near the end of third period.

He said, "Do you want to finish this football season or don't you?"

I let a smile break wide open across my face. In nearly every situation, a smile was my best weapon. Relax. Stay cool. Don't let stuff bother you—that was my philosophy.

You'd be surprised at the number of problems I'd ducked like that, though I admit more and more lately things were starting to irritate me. Like my girlfriend Mindy and the school system's new eligibility policy for athletes.

But, still smiling, I settled my 195 pounds into the straight-back metal chair in front of Coach Maddox's desk and said, "Not to worry, Coach. I've got everything taken care of."

"You understand the new eligibility policy?" he said. He picked up a pencil and tapped the pointed end on his desktop. *Tappity-tap-tap.* He's fifty-five, well built. His craggy face twisted into a scowl as he sat across from me.

"Got to have a C-average to play," I said.

"No Fs." *Tappity-tap-tap.* "Even if you've got a C-average, but you've got an F thrown in, you can't play." *Tappity-tap-tap.*

"That's right," I said and gave a big grin. I was keeping a little secret from him.

He dropped the pencil on his desk and peered at me. "Wipe that smirk off your face and tell me why, after three weeks of school, when I go around this morning to visit your teachers, does Ms. Oberhaus tell me you are failing American Lit?" He smacked the desk with an open palm, and the coffee cup next to his desk calendar jumped. "Tell me!"

I shrugged.

"She doesn't like me," I said. "And she's got this German accent, I can't understand her."

"Hell no, you can't understand her. Not when you sleep in class. She tells me you are doing the same thing in her class this year you did last year—when you failed. NOTHING!"

"Take it easy, Coach."

"Stony, last year the Tigers were a good team. Six and three. That isn't bad. This year we can do better. Conference champs, maybe."

"No doubt."

"State tournament berth, maybe." '

"You bet."

"It's been eight years since we've been in the playoffs. The key is defense."

"We won our first three games," I reminded him, "and have given up only two touchdowns."

"And you've been spectacular. Averaging two sacks a game and ten tackles from your linebacker spot."

"I get lots of help."

"You've blocked four punts and two extra points. Caused four fumbles. Recovered two. Not bad."

I shifted my weight in the chair. I felt funny, the coach complimenting me like this, a very rare thing. "You got nothing to worry about," I told him.

"What happens to the defense when you're not eligible? Tell me that. Mid-quarter reports are out in two-and-a-half weeks. You need at least a D in American Lit. Sixty percent."

"I can handle that."

"But Ms. Oberhaus says your average is thirty-eight percent. You don't read the assignments, write the journal entries, hand in your written work, or study for the tests. You don't do anything, Stony."

"I don't like that stuff, Coach."

"You think I like teaching coed PE? Hell no. But I do it. You understand what I'm saying?"

I shrugged.

"You're lazy, Stony. You got all kinds of potential, but you're lazy. You like math, don't you?"

"It's all right."

"You got an A in math. And you like Creative Foods."

"We get to eat the things we cook."

"History. D-plus."

"Boring."

"Geography: C-minus. Damn near a D."

I finally said, "You don't have to worry about me and American Lit. I'm getting a tutor."

"I know. Ms. Oberhaus told me."

I blinked. I was a little disappointed. My surprise was no surprise at all. "A peer tutor," I said. "It's the HELP program—kids helping other kids learn. Ms. Oberhaus said I should try it."

"That doesn't mean you don't have to work, Stony. You still got to stay awake in class. Read your assignments. Hand in your papers. Pass your quizzes and tests."

"That's true," I said. "But listen, Coach. I'm supposed to meet this girl—Robyn Knight—in the library every day, seventh period, and she's going to help me."

"You still got to get your ass in gear."

"I'll get her to do my work for me," I said. "I won't have any problems at all."

"That isn't how it works, Stony."

But I smiled and said, "Wait and see."

With that I ducked out of Coach Maddox's office. He's a great coach, but he's a worrier, and he gets too emotional, especially on the sidelines during a game, whether we're winning or losing, pacing in front of the bench, yelling and screaming, pounding the air with his fists. Had he relaxed a little, he would have seen that I was perfectly capable of handling my American Lit grade.

• • •

"I can't believe this!" Mindy said. Wide-set in an oval face, her eyes were large and dark. "Everybody's always trying to screw things up for us."

"I can't help it," I said. "If I don't get tutored I'm going to fail American Lit. Then I can't play football."

We were standing in the crowded hall in front of my locker, just after I'd come from Maddox's office. Kids were whipping locker doors open and digging for books, notebooks, pens, and pencils.

Mindy had nearly backed me into my open locker. Only an inch away from me, looking up into my face, she stood with her hands balled into fists on her hips. She was wearing faded jeans and a loose yellow T-shirt.

We'd been going together two years, and I didn't know how to tell her I thought we both needed a change.

"What about our plans for seventh period?" she demanded. Though she's dark complexioned, her face was turning red.

"Don't get excited."

She smelled of cigarette smoke and of the spicy perfume I'd bought for her birthday.

I said, "I'll meet this girl the first couple of times and get her to do my homework. Then maybe I'll see her once or twice a week. We can still skip seventh period a few times."

The thing is, Mindy worked practically every night after school at McDonald's, and I had football practice. This meant we didn't have much time for each other during the week. Unless we could skip seventh period and grab a few minutes to make out.

Lockers banged shut up and down the hallways as kids cleared out, diving into classrooms.

I shifted my books in my arms. "We're going to be late."

"What's this tutor's name?"

"Robyn Knight. Know her?"

Mindy shook her head of reddish brown hair, and her lips turned pouty. "She better be ugly."

two

After lunch, I was sleeping comfortably in fifth-period study hall in the cafeteria, head in the crook of my arm on the table—I loved an after-lunch nap—when I felt someone pulling at my shoulder.

"Mr. Duval wants to see you." Mrs. Larsen, one of the study hall monitors, was shaking me awake.

I rubbed my blurry eyes with my left hand. Shook my right arm. It always went numb and tingled when I slept on it. "What?"

Mrs. Larsen said, "Mr. Duval wants to see you?"

"Who?" I said.

"Your counselor. Remember him?" Then Mrs. Larsen gave me a wry grin and said, "Imagine, you won't get a chance to drool on the tabletop today."

• • •

"Did Ms. Oberhaus tell you we have a tutor ready for you?" Mr. Duval said as I sank into the chair in front of his desk, padded with a maroon seat and back, matching his swivel chair.

I nodded and yawned. Brushed my hand through my short blond hair, bristly on top, a six-inch pigtail curling at the base of my skull.

I never see it, but Mindy said it looked cool and kept it braided for me and decorated it with tiny, colorful beads.

"Robyn Knight." Mr. Duval leaned back in his chair, swiveling back and forth. He was heavyset. Bald. Wore a white shirt and dark tie every day. "Great girl. Brilliant. She wants to be a journalist someday."

I was wondering if she was hot.

"The point is, if you use half your brain, she'll be able to help you. But you can't sit around and do nothing. You understand that?"

I nodded. Yawned again. Still sleepy.

"You can't smile your way through this like you do everything else. You get a failing report at mid-quarter, you can kiss your football season goodbye. Chances are you won't be eligible for the playoffs, either. You understand what I'm saying?"

"I understand."

Mr. Duval scooted his chair closer to his desk. He always spoke in a calm voice, a bit low. You got the impression he knew a lot, and he chose his words carefully to make sure he got them right.

"There's something even more important than football involved here," he said. "What are you going to do with the rest of your life, Wendell?"

I winced, my jaw twisting. Wendell was my real name. Wendell Stoneking. But everyone called me Stony. They called my dad Stony, too. Wendell was my grandpa's first name, my mom's dad. It was an okay name, but not one you'd hang on kids nowadays. When Mr. Duval started calling me Wendell, I knew he was getting serious.

"Tell me," he repeated. "What are you going to do with the rest of your life?"

I shrugged. It was a question he'd asked before, but I still didn't have an answer, mainly because I hadn't given the problem much thought. My future would take care of itself.

"You're a senior," he said. "You could be a good student, if you wanted. Ever think about that?"

I shrugged.

"You're a great football player. There will be scholar-ships out there for your asking. I've told you this a million times."

Another shrug.

"Look at your buddy Brian Hall. He's applied himself in the classroom and on the football field. He doesn't have the physical abilities you do, but he's committed on and off the field. He'll play somewhere."

"Good for him."

Duval said, "I've known your mom and dad since we were kids. We all went to school here. I knew your grandpa. You can work in the gravel pits, too, if you want, a heavy equipment operator, like your grandpa."

"I think I'd like that."

"Maybe be a foreman someday, like your dad. There's nothing wrong with that."

"The money's okay."

"But you should realize there's something different out there for you. If you want it. Do you understand that?"

"Yes, sir."

"You worked in the quarry last summer. You've had a taste of it. Is that what you want?"

Duval was making me a little uncomfortable. I shifted my weight in the padded chair and tried to smile my way through this.

"It's all right," I said.

"Well, now's the time to make up your mind. If you don't do something with your grades this quarter, right now, you'll blow your chance for a football scholarship, probably your only ticket to college."

"But I don't know about college."

"Your dad had the same chance. He was a hell of a high school football player, too, and he ended up in the quarry."

"He's always had a job."

"Nothing wrong with that," Mr. Duval said again, holding up a hand. "Don't get me wrong. But if you want something different in life, now's the time to make your move. Got it?"

"Got it," I said. "Can I go now?"

"Wendell . . ."

"Yes, sir?"

"If you decided to make a change, you can start by staying awake in study halls and in American Lit, by cooperating with Robyn Knight, and by getting an A in lit. In history and geography, too. Take your SATs this spring. You didn't even show up last year."

"Sorry about that."

He said, "Life is about setting goals and making smart choices, Wendell. It's about time you start doing both."

I hustled out of Mr. Duval's office.

I'd never in my life set any goals or made any important choices. I mean, like, who my parents are, where I was born and go to school, what courses I've been taking. All those choices have been made for me. Not even Mindy or football was a conscious goal of mine. Both just happened to me. I didn't set a goal and say to myself *I'm going to be a great football player* or *I'm going to lay Mindy Hillman whenever I can.* All that just happened. Life just happens. You take the good with the bad and try not to sweat anything too much. Especially the bad stuff. It'll drive you crazy. Keep smiling.

· · ·

At first glance, I couldn't decide if Robyn Knight was ugly or not.

Tall and thin, dressed in a black long-sleeved blouse and black flared jeans and combat boots, she strode to the back of the library where I'd been waiting for her. She plunked down the pile of books and folders she was clutching to her chest and pulled out a chair.

We were meeting in a little alcove behind the fiction section where students are allowed to work together quietly. The only one at the table, I slouched in a chair, my arm slung over its back. I was smiling at her. "Hi."

"Hi," she said. "I'm Robyn Knight."

Soft voice. No return smile, though. No offer of a hand-shake. Hardly any boobs. Not like Mindy.

Remaining slouched—relaxed, actually—I broadened my smile until my dimples popped into view. I can't feel them, but I know they punctuate my cheeks—I've seen them in a mirror. And once in tenth grade, before I met Mindy, a preppy girl I liked said my smile was "positively disarming." I looked *disarming* up in a dictionary. It means *winning*.

I said, "You're the tutor?"

"That's right. You're Wendell Stoneking?"

I kept smiling. "Everybody calls me Stony."

She nodded.

Her face was thin with high cheekbones. Her long, straight, pitch-black hair, parted in the middle, hung to her shoulders. As she sat down, she tucked the hair on the right side behind her ear. A long silver earring swung from her earlobe like a pendulum.

"I see you have your book," she said. "But where's your notebook? Do you have a pencil or pen?"

I sat up and flipped open my American Lit book. Tucked in the center of the book were three sheets of folded notebook paper and a stub of pencil, the eraser worn to nothing.

"I'm ready," I said.

"Not quite." She reached for a notebook in the center of the stack of books she'd set on the table. Her fingers were long and thin, nails short, a ring of either silver or turquoise on practically every finger. Even her thumbs. She pulled out a worn spiral notebook with a green cover and held it up. "I took American Lit last year—"

"Me, too," I said.

"—and passed."

I flinched.

"I know for a fact Ms. Oberhaus wants you to keep a notebook like this. Notes about the authors and historical events in the front of the book. A glossary of lit terms in the middle. Journal entries in back."

"Can—*may* I see that?" I held out my hand.

"Sure."

I grinned. This notebook would make things easy. But as I thumbed through its pages, my grin turned to a frown.

George Washington. War of 1812. World War I. The New Deal. Harry S. Truman.

"This isn't American Lit." I slapped the book closed.

"My history notes from last year."

"Where's your lit notes? Did you save them, too?"

"Yes."

"Could I use them? Make things a lot simpler."

She shook her head and her hair spilled out from behind her ear. "You've got to keep your own notebook. I brought my history one to show you what Ms. Oberhaus means by a notebook. A thick one. Three hundred pages with dividers for different sections."

I frowned again.

This wasn't going to be as easy as I'd thought. Robyn Knight looked as if she was all business. Probably genius IQ, 150 or something. Efficient. Picky. I hated girls like that.

I shoved the notebook across the table to her.

"Where do we start?" I said.

"How far are you? What author?"

I shrugged.

She said, "Bradford, Bradstreet, Byrd, Edwards—are you still dealing with the Puritans?"

"I remember flunking that test. I think we're into Poe."

"Not the easiest writer." She leaned closer to me. "Let's see your book." For the first time I caught the delicate scent of her perfume. Her eyebrows were thick and dark, her eyelashes long. She flipped though the pages at the beginning of the text. "Here it is. 'The Masque of the Red Death.' Great story. Is that your assignment?"

For a second I couldn't take my eyes off her.

The long black hair, the colorful rings, the black blouse and jeans, the combat boots, plus all the brains she apparently had—she was a mystery.

"Is that your assignment?" she repeated firmly.

"Um . . . I think so." I looked at the page. "Yeah, I guess that's it."

"Hell," she said. "How do you expect to do well if you're not even sure what the assignments are?"

I felt sheepish.

She said, "First thing you've got to do is read the story. Then to get ready for Ms. Oberhaus's quiz, you've got to write out the answers to the study questions at the end of the story. I don't suppose you have Ms. Oberhaus's lecture notes about Poe."

I shook my head. "Fell asleep that day. I fall asleep every day in her class. The way she talks, I can't understand her."

"You can if you listen closely."

"Look," I said, "tell me what happened in the story. Then tell me the answers to the study questions. I've got a great memory. I'll pass the Poe quiz, no problem."

Robyn latched the hair on both sides of her head behind her ears. Her neck was long and thin. She studied me closely, her hazel eyes penetrating me. I suddenly felt unnerved and squirmed a bit.

"That's not what tutoring is all about," she said coolly. "If you want to pass this course, you're going to do your own work."

Give me a break!

"If you ask Ms. Oberhaus, she'll probably let you write the journal entries you've missed and hand them in late for at least partial credit."

"Only partial credit?"

"If you're lucky. And you'll have to take notes about the other writers you've missed in this unit—Irving, Cooper, and Bryant—so you can pass the next unit test. Then you'll have to stay on top of things for the rest of the semester."

I was starting to feel bewildered.

"For starters," Robyn said, "read Poe's story this class period. Then for homework—"

I felt my frown cutting deeper into my face.

"—write out the answers to the study questions. Bring them with you tomorrow when we meet."

"You're my tutor!" I protested. "What the hell are you going to do? You're making me do *all* the work."

Smiling sweetly, she said, "I'm not the lazy fuck trying to stay eligible for football, Wendell."

Ouch!

. . .

In the boys' locker room, before football practice that afternoon, I plunked down next to Brian Hall on the wooden bench that stretched in front of a row of lockers. I was still smarting from my final exchange with Robyn Knight. What a witch.

The room was jammed with hooting, hollering guys dressing for practice, some fully dressed in pads, some in only a T-shirt or a jockstrap, others in school clothes, digging in their lockers for their smelly gear.

Brian and I'd been best friends in grade school and junior high. We'd grown up in the same little town of Hickory Ridge, Iowa, on the Mississippi River. Population six hundred. A couple of "Hicks from Hickory Ridge"—and proud of it—we now went to Thompsonville High.

There were some big differences between Brian and me, though. Brian's dad was the principal of the grade school we attended in Hickory Ridge. My dad worked in the quarry. Brian studied his ass off in school. I was a screw-off. Brian was the Tigers' offensive leader in football, while I led the defense.

But together we were a great one-two punch.

We didn't hang together much anymore. Mindy didn't like the preppy girls he dated, and his preppy girlfriends didn't like Mindy. Besides, Brain started developing friendships with guys he met in his accelerated classes like chemistry and fourth-year French, friendships that didn't include me. Still, if I was in deep trouble, I knew I could count on Brian.

Already dressed in my muddy, stinking, grass-stained gear, I leaned over to tie my shoes and said to Brian, "How's the elbow?"

He adjusted his shoulder pads under his jersey. Tall, slender as a reed, he had a gun for an arm, but lately, after every game, his elbow was turning up sore.

"The same." He rotated his right arm. Winced. "Stiff. Pain in the elbow that buzzes."

"You popping pain killers?"

That's what he did last summer during baseball season, when the arm bothered him so much.

"Over-the-counter stuff," he said. "Nothing to worry about."

"How many a day?"

He shrugged and swept his hand through his curly blond hair.

"You look pale," I said. "You should try eating more."

"Then I'd be ugly like you."

I smiled and said, "Tell Maddox the arm is bothering you. Maybe he'll give you a week off from practice."

"He'll bench me. If I'm going to play college ball, I need the stats. You know that. Who's going to recruit a six-four quarterback that weighs a hundred-fifty pounds if he doesn't have stats?"

"What's going to happen," I said, "is you're going to end up not being able to throw at all."

He made a face. He didn't like that. "You taking care of your English grade?"

"I'm working on it. Still got your American Lit notes from last year?"

"Might have."

"See if you can dig them up."

"Lit's not hard. All you've got to do is read the stuff. Do the assignments."

"Notes would help." I finally tied my other shoe.

"I'll see what I can do. Tried a tutor?"

"Got one."

"Who?"

"Robyn Knight."

Smiling, he leaned back against his locker door. "I work with her on the newspaper staff. She transferred here from out of state last year. Lives with her sister, I think."

"She smart?"

"She's so smart she's weird. She wrote a piece about girls who are abused by their boyfriends—a lot of them jocks. Won a national award."

Brain picked up his helmet from the floor and stood, ready to leave.

I said, "Look for your notes, will you?"

"Right. Probably got them somewhere." He squeezed his helmet onto his head and snapped the strap. "We need you on defense, Stony. You're the man. Don't screw up."

"And we need you on offense, dumbshit. Have someone look at that arm."

I pawed through the junk on the top shelf of my locker for my mouthpiece.

"One other thing about Robyn Knight," he said. "She's got a kid. Logan is his name, I think."

That announcement halted my hand in the middle of its search. A girl in high school having a baby isn't anything unusual. Happens all the time. But for some reason, Robyn Knight, with all her brains, didn't seem the type.

When I turned to ask Brain if he was kidding about the baby, he was already heading out of the locker room, jabbering with his offensive center, flexing his right arm, still trying to loosen up the elbow.

Robyn Knight was a very bright, unwed mother. A no-nonsense geek who probably hated jocks, she was my tutor. An eerie feeling crept over me. I knew I was going to have trouble with this skinny do-gooder.

three

After football practice, my radio cranked to the max with country and western, window down, I headed home in my pride and joy, my old Ford pickup. Manual transmission. Newly painted light green, the truck had been my grandpa Stoneking's. Everyone called him Stony, too.

The sun was still bright and warm. I drove south along a five mile stretch of Highway 22, a four-lane that runs parallel to the Mississippi River. The river wasn't visible from the highway, though, because industrial plants with tall chimneys belching smoke blocked the view.

Like I said, I lived in Hickory Ridge, Iowa, a tiny village a few miles south of Thompsonville on the Mississippi. The limestone quarry where Dad worked as a foreman loomed a mile ahead, and already the still air was thick with limestone dust. The quarry was an ugly hole a half mile square and hundreds of feet deep into the earth's belly, where bulldozers, cranes, trucks, and men labored to haul limestone to the surface. If you stood at the quarry's edge and looked down, the trucks and men scattered and scurrying at the bottom look like toys.

As I drove by, the quarry dust filtering into my nostrils, I wondered if I really wanted to work there the rest of my life.

What did Mr. Duval tell me this afternoon?

. . . you should realize there's another life out there for you. Something different—whatever it might be. If you want it. Do you understand that?

But it was hard to imagine I'd do anything different with my life from what my grandpa and dad had done. The quarry had been good enough for them.

On my left, only thirty yards away, clear now of factories, the Mississippi flowed, a mile wide and glassy in the sunshine. Soo Line railroad tracks ran parallel to the Mississippi through Hickory Ridge. Trains rumbled by once or twice a day. Their sound always sent a shiver through me. I didn't like to think about trains. A train killed my younger brother Shane.

On my right, facing the railroad tracks and the river, the painted store fronts of what was Hickory Ridge's two-block business section huddled together as if to protect themselves from the wind, rain, and snow that blew in from the river. The only brick building in town was the new bank.

My mom's bait and tackle shop—called Stony's—sat at the south end of the street. I pulled my truck up in front of the place and jumped out. A blue Tahoe pulling a Lund with a fifty-horse Johnson was also parked on the side in the gravel lot. As I opened the screen door to the bait shop and stepped in, a bell tinkled above my head.

Mom stood behind the counter, ringing up a sale of dew worms, stink bait, treble hooks, and sinkers for two city fishermen. They were just leaving, and I held the door. "Good luck, men," I said.

Mom fixed me with a stare, her eyes blue as sky. "See your dad's truck at Foggy's?"

I often wondered if she was a fox in high school like Mindy. I think she was. She still had a shape, but her face showed age—wrinkles at the corners of her eyes and mouth, shadows under her eyes. Her dark hair was streaked with gray, too.

"Didn't look," I said honestly, but I knew it was probably parked there.

"Air compressor for the minnow tank is acting up again. Going to lose a bunch like last time unless he fixes it right."

"I'll try to get him."

Mom shook her head. "Could use some help around here. Getting so I can't stand the sight of the place."

"I'll work for you Sunday, Mom." I often did that so she could have a day off.

Though small, the bait shop was neatly kept and organized. Hooks, sinkers, lures, rods, reels, tackle boxes, nets—every piece of equipment was in its place, thanks to Mom. The back room housed the live bait tanks and a refrigerator for shrimp, worms, and chicken livers.

Mom said, "Get your dad."

"I'll try."

Outside, I climbed into my truck.

My mom and dad went together at Thompsonville High. Same as Mindy and me. Mom and Dad married right after graduation. I suspect that's what Mindy has in mind for us because lately she's been slipping the idea into our conversation whenever possible.

• • •

Dad was shooting pool.

I watched from a stool at the bar. Foggy, the bartender, poured me a tall glass of Pepsi with ice in it. Dad was the best pool shooter in town. Best picks shooter and euchre player, too.

I knew better than to speak to Dad when he was drawing down on the eight ball.

"You kids going to win Friday night?" Foggy peered at me from behind the bar though his thick glasses.

"We're going to win them all," I said. "State champs."

"Can I bet on that?"

"Bet the bar, the farm, the car, the boat—whatever you want. We'll be state champs."

Quarry workers lined the bar. A few sat at tables, playing cards. An old Waylon Jennings tune rattled the jukebox, and cigarette smoke drifted in the air. You could always spot the quarry workers. A film of gray dust clung to their billed caps, T-shirts, jeans, and boots. Grey dust clung to their eyebrows, beards, mustaches, and the hair of their arms.

Dad stroked.

Lots of green. Tough angle.

The cue ball slashed the eight ball, and the money-ball *plunked* into the corner pocket.

Smiling, Dad plucked two five-dollar bills off the bar, the five he'd bet and the five he'd won. "Next?" Dad glanced up and down the bar. No one volunteered. When he spied me, his face burst into a smile, a lot like mine does, people say. "What are you doing here? Your ma send you?"

"Air compressor for the minnow tank isn't working right. She's afraid a bunch of minnows are going to die."

"Nothing wrong with the compressor. She doesn't keep the filter clean, that's the problem."

"She wants you to look at it, anyway."

Dad squeezed my shoulder. "You eat yet?"

I shook my head.

"Foggy!" Dad called. "Double cheeseburger and fries here. You eat, and I'll give you a pool lesson."

"What about Mom?"

"She knows how to clean the filter."

• • •

At eight-thirty, Mom stomped into Foggy's, the screen door banging closed behind her. I was coming back from the restroom. I stopped in my tracks in front of the jukebox, then approached my folks cautiously. Neither one saw me.

Foggy set a glass of draft in front of Mom without her asking.

"Thought I sent Wendell to get you." Mom stared at Dad.

"He's here someplace."

"He tell you what I wanted?"

"All you got to do is keep the filter clean."

"It's not the damned filter. By morning I'm not going to have one minnow left." Mom drank half her beer and wiped her mouth with the back of her hand.

"I'll look at it," Dad said.

"When?" Mom gulped the rest of her beer and Foggy slid another one in front of her on the bar before she lowered her glass. "When you can't see?"

That's when I turned slowly and slipped out of Foggy's back door.

I'd watched that scenario before. Both Mom and Dad would come home screaming and cussing at each other, Dad breaking things he fell into, Mom breaking things she threw at him.

It happened once or twice a month. Mostly twice, lately.

• • •

I drove home.

Darkness had settled. Streetlights glowed over each intersection. Crickets chirped. Three blocks away Vernon Purdy's coonhound howled mournfully.

I lived with Mom and Dad four blocks up the street from Foggy's. Our house was an old two-story wooden-framed structure on a corner, with badly peeling white paint, rotting shingles, and a sagging front porch.

When the phone rang at eleven o'clock, I was lying on the lumpy couch in the living room, trying to watch TV and read the "Masque of the Red Death" a third time.

It was the first thing I'd read for American Lit all year, and it was hard. Long paragraphs. Big words. I could handle that, though, if I really worked at it. It was just a lot of bother.

I found the cordless phone in the lounge chair, half stuffed under the cushion.

I flopped back on the couch.

"Hi," Mindy said. "What are you doing?" She always called when she got off work at McDonald's. If she could wrestle the phone away from her mom.

"Watching TV and reading a story for lit tomorrow."

"Your tutor, Robyn Knight—"

"What about her?"

"—is a druggie."

"Who told you that?"

"Debbie. She pointed her out to me at school. Says that's why she wears long-sleeved shirts and blouses all the time, to hide needle tracks."

Debbie Nicholson was a girl Mindy worked with at McDonald's.

"Get real," I said.

"She's got lots of tattoos, too. Some girls have seen her in the shower after PE."

"You shouldn't listen to rumors, Mindy."

"Ask her tomorrow. Ask to see her arms. What did you think of her?"

"She's smart."

"You like her?"

"Of course not."

"I missed you seventh period," Mindy whispered. She had this sultry voice she used on the phone sometimes that always sent shivers down my spine. "Want me to talk dirty? Where are you? In the living room? Lay down on the couch."

Mindy was really good at talking like that over the phone. I think it was something she'd learned from her mom, a motorcycle broad with lots of tattoos herself and a pierced tongue. Mindy sported one tattoo, a snake on her left breast, and a pierced belly button.

I said, "Not tonight, babe. I've got to read this story again. I don't think my tutor's going to do my homework for me."

"Please . . ."

"Honest, I can't."

"Don't you dare hang up," she said. "Not for some stupid story."

"Sorry. Gotta go. Got to stay eligible."

"Stony!"

"See you tomorrow."

I punched the OFF button on the cordless. I waited for the phone to ring, Mindy calling back to scream at me. But when it didn't ring, I knew she was pissed. When she got that way, she wouldn't talk. It was like she blew a fuse or something. She'd been doing that a lot lately.

After I finished Poe's story a third time, I trudged upstairs to my room, undressed and flopped on my squeaky bed in my jockey shorts in the dark. My window was open, a soft breeze blowing in and rustling the curtains, a splash of moonlight pooling on the floor.

My folks wouldn't be home until about 1:00 AM. Foggy never kicked them out until he'd let them spend their money, or he was tired of their bickering.

I thought of the quarry and of my mom and dad and of Mindy and me and again of what Mr. Duval said to me today, ". . . *another life out there . . . Something different . . .*"

I wondered if I really could have a life different from my folks' life. What would it be like? Would it be without Mindy?

"Life is about setting goals and making smart choices, Wendell."

Was I starting to worry? I hoped not.

The last thing I remembered before falling asleep was the sound of Vernon Purdy's coonhound baying at the moon, the mournful wail floating in through my open window, as I was thinking, *What goals should I set? What choices should I make?*

I was eighteen—I started school late and flunked first grade—and I didn't have a clue.

four

The next morning, in front of Mindy's locker before school, she said, "Are we going to skip seventh?"

Kids dashed by, heading for classrooms.

"Can't," I said. "Got to meet my tutor."

"You hang up on me last night because you've got to read a stupid story. You can't skip seventh because you've got to meet with your tutor. What's going on, Stony?"

"Big quiz tomorrow. Poe. Got to be ready."

Then with a coy smile Mindy said, "Can you skip half of seventh period?" She curled a lock of hair around her finger. "What I have in mind won't take long."

"Not today. Friday." I glanced at my watch. "We've got to split."

• • •

That afternoon, I met Robyn in the back of the library at the same secluded table. It felt hot in the corner, and the air seemed stuffy. In front of me, on the table, sat my American Lit text and a three-hundred-page spiral notebook.

I said, "We have a mutual friend—Brian Hall. Works with you on the newspaper staff."

"I know Brian," she said. "I wouldn't say we're friends."

"You don't like him?"

"He's a little pushy sometimes."

"He's aggressive," I said. "That's what makes him a good quarterback."

She was wearing practically the same outfit today that she had worn yesterday. Black jeans. Combat boots. Only today she was wearing a man's dark-flannel shirt with a collar and long sleeves. Gold hoop earrings.

"I mentioned you're my tutor. He said you're smart."

"That's all?"

I didn't want to say anything about her having a kid, so I said, "We both come from Hickory Ridge—little town ten miles down the road from here. I'm kind of the defensive leader in football. He takes charge of the offense."

Apparently not interested in football, she nodded briefly and said, "Let's get to work. I see you bought a notebook. That's good. Did you read the story?"

"Three times."

"What did you think?"

"Cool."

"Tell me what happened."

I thought a moment. "Well, all these medieval guys are trying to escape the Red Death, a disease that if you catch it, makes you bleed to death, like you're sweating through your pores. This prince—"

"What's the prince's name?"

I thought again. "Prospero. This Prince Prospero locks himself up in a castle with a bunch of other people who don't have the disease. The idea is to keep the disease out and to keep himself and everyone else in the castle safe."

"Very good. What happens?"

"Well, after a time everyone gets cabin fever. So Prospero throws a big party. A masquerade ball. A kegger. One guy shows up dressed like the Red Death. The prince is pissed—" I halted and cleared my throat. "Sorry."

"Go on."

"Well, when Prospero tries to unmask the guy who's dressed like the Red Death, he finds out that the guy isn't wearing a mask at all. He *is* the Red Death. He got in. All the party people, the prince included, fall onto the floor in pools of their own blood and bleed to death." I nodded and crossed my arms, satisfied with my synopsis. "It was pretty cool. What will Ms. Oberhaus's questions be?"

"I don't know. I'm sure she changes them from semester to semester. Did you write out the answers to the study questions?"

I shook my head. "I was going to do it in study hall. I started." I flipped open my notebook to the first page where I'd written a partial answer to the first question. "I fell asleep," I said, and smiled, hoping she'd be impressed with my honesty.

"You fall asleep on the football field, too?" she said.

"Never."

"I suggest you stay awake in the classroom—if you want to continue playing football."

This skinny broad was lecturing me. I felt miffed but tried to hide it with another smile and said, "I will, I promise."

"Check out the third question. Ms. Oberhaus always asks questions about allegory. You know what that means?"

"A story where they use symbols and stuff. Gives the story some kind of hidden meaning."

"A story in which people, objects, or events act as symbols, often revealing a truth about reality."

"That's what I said."

"What do you think Poe's story says about reality?"

I frowned. Scratched my head. "I don't know . . . I've got an idea, I guess, but it's stupid."

"Tell me."

I shrugged. "No matter how hard you try, bad things are bound to happen to you. You can't escape evil in the world, you have to face reality. You can't run."

I thought of Brian trying to escape the fact his elbow was giving him trouble. Of my reluctance to tell Mindy we should split. Of my failure to make any decisions about my life. Set any goals.

Robyn sat back in her chair and looked at me. I felt like she was appraising me, like she was checking out a car. Inspecting the paint job. Looking for rust, nicks, dents. "Not bad," she said.

"Thanks."

"Can you apply any of what you just said to your own life?"

"Um . . . I can't escape my poor lit grade. And if I don't improve, I might bleed to death of my own stupidity."

She gave a little nod. "If Ms. Oberhaus asks a question about allegory, you might include that. She'll be impressed."

"All right."

Robyn picked up a notebook of her own and thumbed it open. "You'll be having a unit test shortly. Probably the beginning of next week—Monday. Not much time. You've got to get to work right away."

"I will."

"You haven't got notes about any of the authors in this unit, have you?"

"I haven't got notes about any authors."

She shoved her notebook across the table to me. "Irving, Cooper, Bryant, Poe—you can copy my notes about those guys this period. You'll have to work fast."

"I could photocopy them."

"Uh-uh. Copy them. Then I know you've read the material at least once. For the rest of the year, you'll have to keep your own notes."

Again I felt miffed. She was treating me like a damned kid.

"Over the weekend," she said, "you should read all the selections from this unit that you haven't read. And study your notes."

As I listened to her, my eyes narrowed. She wasn't going to let up.

"Do all that," she said, "and you might have a chance to pass the test. Have you asked Ms. Oberhaus about making up journal entries?"

"Not yet."

"Do that, too. She'll be impressed with your sincerity. Write them over the weekend. Maybe she'll give you full credit."

"Anything else I should do over the weekend?" I said. "Like run around the world twice?"

"That's up to you," she said, her hazel eyes clear and cool. "Why don't you copy my notes first?"

five

The entire varsity football team crowded into the boys' locker room after school. Forty-five guys. They didn't make a sound. Not even a whisper.

Coach Maddox stood in our midst on a metal folding chair.

Everyone seemed stunned. No one could believe what Coach Maddox was saying. Could we all be dreaming the same nightmare?

My throat ached.

Brian Hall, our potential all-state quarterback, our offensive leader, was in intensive care at Genesis West Hospital. His folks had called 911 during the night. Some kind of internal bleeding. Nobody knew what caused it.

Pivoting on the chair, catching everyone's eye, Maddox said, "We've got a game tomorrow tonight. We've got to fight through this. And if every man here lays his heart on the line, we *can* fight through it!"

"Is Brian going to be okay?" someone shouted.

"Don't know," Maddox said. "I think so. Once they get the bleeding stopped—and find out what caused it."

Lots of mumbling. Nodding of heads.

"Can we visit him?"

"Not in intensive care," Maddox said. "Only family."

"We'll buy him a card! Everyone sign it."

"Hell! Everyone buy him a card and send it!"

"We'll win for Brian!" someone yelled.

"You bet we'll win for Brian," Maddox said. "And now how about a silent prayer for him."

Everyone's head bowed, his chin nearly touching his chest. I swallowed hard, trying to get rid of the ache in my throat.

Jesus, Brian, what have you done to yourself with those pills?

• • •

When I trotted onto the practice field that afternoon under a gray, cloudy sky, helmet in hand, Maddox stopped me and slung an arm around my shoulder.

"You taking care of that classroom matter, Stony?"

"Yes, sir."

"We got a big problem here. A quarterback that's sidelined. A linebacker that might not be eligible. Team leaders."

"I understand."

"I got four other guys fighting to stay eligible, but it's you I'm worried about." Maddox squeezed my neck, his arm an iron clamp. "Don't let me down."

"I'm going to study all weekend for a test." I squirmed. Scrunched my shoulders. "And make up a bunch of missed work, too."

"All right. Listen to me now." Maddox released his grip on my neck and stood in front of me. I'd never seen him look so pained, so serious, not even when we went 2-7 when I was a sophomore.

"Lunardi is a good quarterback, but he's only a sophomore. Never started a varsity game. He'll be nervous and tight tomorrow night."

"No doubt."

"We could always count on Brian to go out there relaxed and throw on the very first down. Attack. Keep our opponents off balance."

I smiled at the thought of Brian hurling completion after completion down the field. Twenty, thirty yards at a time.

"That's how we've been winning," Maddox said. "Getting an early jump. We can't do that tomorrow night. You understand me?"

I nodded and stared at the top of my scarred, grass-stained helmet.

"So more than ever the defense has got to be tough from the get-go. Pleasant View is a good team. Two-one on the season. They're not going to play dead for us."

"I know that."

"The defense has got to go out there fired up. Ten other guys play defense, but you're their leader. They'll follow your key. What you do, they'll do. You hear me?"

"Yes, sir."

"All right!" He smacked me on the shoulder pad with the heel of his hand and said, "Give me a hundred and ten percent tomorrow night. It's our home game."

"Right."

"I'm counting on you."

"I won't let you down, Coach."

"One other thing."

"What?"

"What's up with Brian? You're his buddy. Internal bleeding, what's that all about? He got an ulcer or something?"

I kicked at the grass.

"I don't know," I lied, wanting to tell him about Brian's arm and the pills Brian had been taking—but not wanting to rat him out. Doctors would figure out in the hospital soon enough what was wrong with him, wouldn't they?

"He's been looking dragged out lately," Maddox said, shaking his head. "A little peaked. I don't know what to make of it. Doesn't seem to be anything wrong with his arm, though."

"He'll be okay."

"Yeah," Maddox said. "Well, you get your ass in gear. Classroom and football field."

. . .

The next day, Friday, the day of my Poe quiz, I burst into the library and back to the table where Robyn sat waiting for me and said, "I think I might've aced Poe. Got a B for damn sure."

Robyn put a finger to her mouth. "Shhh! Not so loud. If they think we're fooling around back here, they won't let us work together."

I whipped out a chair, dropped my books on the table, and sat down. "I know. Did you hear what I said?"

"Yes. And now you see what a little work can accomplish."

A brilliant thought flashed through my brain. I said, "Um . . . look. This might sound pretty stupid . . . but would you . . . well, could you help me study over the weekend? Like maybe Saturday afternoon?"

"I don't think so."

"I've got to make sure I stay eligible. Listen to this . . ."

Then I told her about Brian's going down, not about his sore elbow and his taking pills, though, just about his internal bleeding, and she said, "That's terrible. What do you think it is?"

"No one's sure. But he might be out for a while. I can't afford to fail and I've got to play even better on defense."

"You can study by yourself."

I gave her my big smile. Dimples included.

"Look," I said, "I'd like to copy the notes I missed from the first unit. Bradford, Bradstreet—those guys. I'll have to know that stuff if I'm going to pass the semester evaluation. Right?"

"Unless you do, you won't have a chance."

"You don't want me to photocopy the stuff. So you can watch me copy it word for word—"

"Wouldn't that be fun."

"—then drill me later."

"I don't think so," she said again.

I bit my bottom lip. My mind raced.

"I'll pay you," I said. "Double minimum wage. Even more. What do you think?"

She regarded me thoughtfully, tucking her hair behind her right ear. "I don't know."

"You name your price."

"Like fifteen dollars an hour?" she said.

"It's a deal."

She looked a me doubtfully. "Where would you get that kind of money?"

"I've been working since I was nine. Cutting grass. Shoveling snow. Detasseling corn. Driving a forklift at the quarry."

Again she looked at me, her eyes a little narrow, probably wondering if she could trust me.

"I'll pay you up front," I said. "Three hours' worth."

She twisted a turquoise ring on her thumb around and around. "Where would we go?"

"Libraries are pretty dull," I said.

"We can't go to my house."

"Mine either."

I never brought friends to my house. I never knew when my folks might be drunk and fighting. Besides, the house was nearly always too much of a wreck inside to invite anyone over.

"I've got the perfect place," I said. "Outdoors. Quiet. Peaceful. Nothing but sunshine, trees, birds, and a breeze."

"A park?"

I nodded. "Out in the country."

Her eyes brightened, and for the first time I saw her wide lips curve into a smile.

"All right," she said. "I'd like that."

"Great!"

We settled on one o'clock tomorrow afternoon, and she told me where she lived. When we shook hands on the deal, I realized that she was again wearing a long-sleeved flannel shirt.

Was she really hiding needle tracks on her arms? How many tattoos did she have? Why was she living with her sister?

She apparently needed money.

•   •   •

Mindy met me at my truck in the parking lot. I was sitting inside, waiting, tapping my foot on the floorboard. She wore cutoff bibs, a yellow tube top underneath. We met every Friday like this before a game. Even away games. School was out at 2:35, and I didn't have report to the locker room until 3:30.

Most guys dived into a fast-food place for something to eat.

I met with Mindy. Oral sex. Before every game. Mindy's gift of good luck. Her special favor.

She said, "Hey. Been waiting long?"

"Ten minutes."

The front seat of my pickup is a bench seat long enough for three people, complete with seat belts, so there was no awkward gearshift or anything else between us.

As I drove to the park where we always settled down, hidden in a grove of oak trees, she scooted over and snuggled close, wrapping her arms around my neck, kissing me.

"I missed you." Her tongue flicked my ear lobe. A little shiver shot through me, as if a fly was pestering me. *Scat.*

I drove by the park's ball diamonds, tennis courts, and kiddy playgrounds. Leaving the park behind, the road wound through a woods, leaves beginning to change from green to yellow, brown, and red. I rolled the window down. The air smelled of autumn.

When I pulled up fifteen feet off the road into the woods under our favorite oak tree, Mindy said, "Alicia's throwing a party Saturday night. Her parents are gone. It'll be wild." Mindy kissed me again. And again. She liked tongue-twisting kisses, but I couldn't get into it lately. I wondered what had happened to the overwhelming excitement I felt when we first started making out as sophomores. My blood always felt on fire, and my groin twitched.

The rush had vanished, that's all I knew.

"What's wrong?" Mindy said. "Lost your tongue?"

"Mindy—" I pulled my head back. Gulped for air. Banged my head on the door frame. "I passed an American

Lit quiz this morning. First time this year. I might've even gotten an A."

"C'mon, Stony. We're not here to talk about school. Get serious."

"Poe's not easy. I answered a question about allegory."

"Stony!" Her hand roamed near my zipper.

I caught her wrist. "Don't . . ."

"Stony, c'mon!"

"I need to talk to you," I said.

"Now's not the time, sweetie. Later."

I felt her smoky breath on my face and smelled her spicy perfume.

I pushed her away. Her cheeks were flushed.

I said, "I've got to get serious about school. About studying. A lot of people are counting on me."

"That's bullshit."

"It's not. I'm not sure I want to party Saturday night. Or even tonight after the game."

She stared at me. "What's really bothering you?"

"American Lit, I'm telling you. Staying eligible for football."

And what I'm going to do with the rest of my life?

Mindy ran the palm of her hand across the top of my bristly hair, then toyed with the pigtail at the base of my neck.

All right, I admit it. My blood started to tingle just a little.

"I can make you forget all that." Mindy's hand crept to my zipper. "I've waited for this all day."

"Mindy—"

"Shhhh." Her mouth was puckering.

• • •

The night of the game was clear and cold, no wind, a perfect September night for football. Before the game, Coach Maddox gathered us players around in the locker room and said he'd heard from Brian's parents. Brian was doing okay—doctors had pumped him full of blood. He was weak and would have to stay in ICU for a couple more days. No one was sure yet what was wrong with him. He'd be back to school in a week or so. Back on the team.

Everyone else cheered, but I hung my head.

I was the only one who knew about Brian's elbow—him popping pills.

Once the game started, it turned into a dogfight, neither team having much to scream about in the first quarter. Pleasant View, with its huge hunks of meat on the line, smothered our rookie quarterback, Matt Lunardi. Charger linemen sacked him three times. Twice they tackled him in the backfield before he could hand off. When he did hand off successfully, running backs failed to hit the hole or there was no hole. It was as if the offense couldn't perform without Brian.

A couple of times, PV blasted the ball into our territory. But I'm proud to say rugged gang tackling, dogged pursuit, and a couple of last-second desperation tackles kept PV out of the end zone. The defense was kicking ass.

On the sidelines Coach Maddox was going berserk, grimacing, screaming himself hoarse at the offense, "Block! Somebody block!"

Standing on the sidelines next to the coach, I was wondering how much longer our defense could hang on. Sweat dripped down my face, and I was breathing like I'd run a hundred miles, sucking great gulps of the crisp night air into my lungs. My bottom lip was split open, and I could taste blood.

When we hustled in again on defense, near the middle of the second period, PV took the ball over on its own forty-five after one of our many hurried punts.

The Chargers' first play from scrimmage looked like an end run, their quick, 175-pound tailback sweeping to the short side of the field.

But I diagnosed the play. They couldn't fool me, even if I was still out of breath from our last defensive stand. The play was a reverse, their speedy flanker taking the hand off from the tailback, hoping to race to the wide side of the field, outrunning everyone.

I knifed in behind the line, dove for the flanker's legs, and snagged one, slowing him up a second. But *goddamn!* I didn't hook the other leg. The flanker ripped free of my one-armed tackle, leaving me buried helmet-first in the dirt and grass. The flanker swept wide, turned the corner, and flew down the sideline for a touchdown, untouched except for my missed tackle. *Jesus!*

The game was different after that.

Pleasant View scored again in the second quarter for a 14-0 lead at halftime.

Even Coach Maddox's impassioned plea at halftime for the Tigers to ". . . regroup . . . lay your hearts on the line . . . win for Brian . . ." couldn't change things.

We played like zombies during the second half, dead people moving in slow motion. PV scored two touchdowns in the third and posted its final TD with thirty seconds left in the game on a forty-yard pass. Not a single Tiger touched the PV passer or the receiver.

After the Tiger kicker booted the ball through the goal posts for the point after the touchdown, the final score was 35-0. An ass kicking.

I was devastated.

Our offense had folded, and our defense had collapsed. We'd all played like shit.

Helmet hooked and dangling from the fingers of my right hand, head bowed, blood dripping from my nose and my lip, sweat running down my face, I felt tears bursting from my eyes as I trudged off the field, the taste of blood and defeat bitter in my mouth.

I had never before cried over winning or losing a football game. The last time I cried was at my brother's funeral, hoping the tears would wash my guilt away, but they didn't.

But losing this game, my missing a tackle that opened the floodgates for PV—I couldn't handle it. When I reached the sidelines, before anyone saw them, I tried to swipe the tears away with the heel of my hand. I hoped everyone would think my tears were sweat. But I think all I did was smear mud around my stupid-ass face.

Sorry, Brian. We tried our best. I blew it.

SIX

Clinging to me in my truck, Mindy kept her mouth shut on the way to the after-game Romp in the Woods.

The Romp really wasn't a party. Just a meeting of kids that hung together after home games. Some football players. A few cheerleaders. Several girl jocks from the volleyball and softball teams. Guys from basketball and wrestling. Band kids, too. A few preppies and geeks. Regular kids. Tiger football fans.

Usually in my truck, after a game, Mindy and I talked, laughed, joked. Kissed. Rehashed the game. Kissed. But not tonight. This night was different from all other Friday nights this season. We'd lost a game we were expected to win. I'd screwed up.

Besides, my lip was split, and kissing Mindy made my lip hurt even worse.

That night, I made ten tackles. Batted a pass. Recovered a fumble. But I missed the most important tackle of the game. Somehow I'd let up. Missed that guy's other leg. If the defense had shut the Chargers down on that drive, I swear we would have continued to kick ass. Hadn't Maddox told me I was the key to the defense? What I did, the rest of the guys would do. Turned out he was right.

It was eleven o'clock.

The night air was cold, chilling me. The sky was clear, moon and stars shining.

The Romp was in the country, off a gravel road, down a dirt lane to a clearing in a woods where you could build a bonfire, drink a couple of beers, cook hot dogs, bratwurst, and hamburgers. You could crank up your car or truck stereo as loud as you wanted, all hidden from the prying eyes and ears of parents and cops.

The land was posted, but the owner lived out of state. Most kids were good about bagging their garbage and taking it back to to dump in the school dumpster. The neighboring farmer didn't harass anybody by calling the cops because he himself didn't want the kids harassing him.

Didn't want his fences cut, his cows let out, his corn trampled.

Mindy's left hand rested on my right leg. I felt the heat of her hand through my jeans, but I was absolutely not interested in any of her moves tonight.

I wondered if I'd ever recover from our losing the game. My missing a tackle.

I couldn't let myself worry about it. *Keep smiling.*

"The loss wasn't your fault," Mindy finally said in a small voice. Her warmth did feel good next to me.

"We lost concentration," I said. "Maddox told us to go home and forget about it. Sometimes things like that just happen."

She squeezed my leg. "I'll help you forget about it."

"Don't . . ."

"I love you, Stony," she whispered.

My old truck bounced over a pothole in the dirt road snaking through the woods, headlights knifing through the darkness. I hit another pothole. I made a face. Pain clawed my ribs on my left side.

But I didn't even think about taking a pill. Like Brian.

I saw the fire flickering through the trees, then smelled the woody smoke. As soon as I stopped my truck at the edge of the clearing and climbed out, I was sorry I'd come. While Mindy scooted to get us a beer, kids crowded around me to congratulate me on a great game. Said under the circumstances the team played as well as could be expected. The loss meant nothing. We could bounce back. It wasn't the end of the season. Or the world.

I hated being patronized.

"Losing wasn't nobody's fault," Dale Higgins said, a guy who played drums in the school band. "Those guys were good."

"How's Brian?" Sheila Arnold asked me, Higgins' girlfriend. Math geek.

"Coach said he's going to be okay," I said.

Then I listened to the conversation fly back and forth.

"What's wrong with him?"

"Internal bleeding."

"What causes that?"

"Nobody seems to know."

"Got to be something."

"Makes you wonder about him, doesn't it?"

"What's that mean?"

"Maybe he's doing drugs."

"Bullshit. He's too smart for that."

"You don't bleed in the stomach from drugs anyway."

"From taking too many aspirin you can. My grandpa did after his knee surgery. He nearly died."

"We'll win big next week," Bobby Vancil, an offensive tackle, said to me. "Right, Stony?"

"Right," I said. "We're survivors."

Mindy hustled back from the cooler with two beers, delivering a cold one to my hand. "For you, baby."

"Thanks."

We crowded around the fire. About twenty of us. Fueled with split logs, the flames leaped and danced into the night, casting a red glow across everyone's face, brightly lighting their eyes and the beer cans they clutched. My front was toasty warm from the fire, but my backside was cold, and my ribs hurt like crazy.

I took a long drink. The beer felt good sliding down my throat into my belly, and the cold can felt good on my split and swollen lip.

Not much chatter among us tonight. No singing at all. Our eyeballs staring into the fire, we were still too numb from the loss and the worry about Brian for a real celebration.

"You want another beer?" Mindy asked me, as she held hers upside down and shook the last drops out of the can. The first two or three she always gulped down.

"Tastes good," I said, "but I don't feel like it tonight. Had only a couple of swallows out of this."

"What do you feel like doing?"

"Not that."

"You will," she said, and smiled. "Then I'll cook you a giant hamburger."

She grabbed my hand and pulled me back to my truck, where I leaned against the fender in the darkness. Away from the fire, I felt cold all over again, especially my butt against the metal fender.

An owl hooted in a faraway tree.

"I'm serious," I said. "I don't feel like doing anything tonight. I don't know why we drove out here."

"I do."

"I don't want to be with these guys. I mean, like, I don't want to talk about that stupid game. Or about Brian."

"I know why we drove out here."

"Not tonight, babe."

Reaching to circle my neck with her arms, she pulled my head down, pressed her body against mine, and kissed me on the corner of the mouth because she knew my lip was split in the center.

I should have started grinding against her now, getting her hotter, but I didn't.

She frowned. "What's wrong?"

"Is this all you ever think about?"

She kissed me again, other corner of my mouth. Took my hand and slipped it inside her denim jacket, under her blouse against her warm flesh.

"It's all we do," I said.

"I love you, Stony. I want to make you happy. That's all I ever want."

I let my hand slip away from her nipple.

"Your ribs still sore? Let me kiss them." She started pulling my shirt out of my jeans. "Did you bring a blanket? A sleeping bag for the back of your truck?"

"No."

"I'll be glad when we're married and have our own bed."

I flinched. There it was, Mindy tossing the idea of marriage into our conversation.

"I'll get a blanket from somebody," she said.

"We're going home."

She pulled back and looked at me in dismay.

"Don't you get it?" I said. "I don't want to be here. I have to study for a unit test all weekend. I need some sleep. I'm going home to bed."

"Study? Sleep?" She stomped her foot. "Since when do you worry about study and sleep on a Friday night?"

"Robyn said I needed to read all the assignments I missed—"

"Robyn?"

"Robyn Knight."

"*She's* on your mind?"

"She's *not* on my mind. She just told me what I had to do, if I want to pass the unit test in lit."

"To hell with her."

"Our whole team has to make up for that loss. Me especially."

"Fuck you, Stony."

I reached for the door on my side of the truck. "C'mon, I don't want to leave you here alone."

"If football's more important than I am—then *go!* I'm staying!"

I doubted if she meant that, but I put her to the test, saying, "Then stay!"

"You prick!"

She gasped when I climbed into my truck and she realized I wasn't kidding.

"Stony!" she shrieked, throwing her hands up at the sky.

But I drove away through the dark woods and never looked back.

seven

When I picked Robyn up Saturday afternoon in front of her sister's house, she was standing at the curb. Seeing me arrive in an old Ford pickup, she tilted her head in surprise.

I figured she thought all jocks drove sporty little cars with chrome wheels. I sat back in my truck, equally surprised to see her standing there with a youngster in her arms, a canvas bag of toys slung over her shoulder, and a car seat on the ground by her feet.

I'd forgotten Brian had told me she had a kid.

"You don't mind if Logan comes along, do you?" she said, as she buckled the boy between us in his car seat in my truck. She placed the canvas bag on the floor by her feet. "I don't get a chance to take him out much. Only to the grocery store. Or the mall."

"I don't mind at all."

Out of the canvas bag she plucked a floppy black-felt hat and plunked it on her head. A black ribbon pulled her black hair back into a ponytail.

I looked down at Logan's round face with its sparkly blue eyes and remembered my little brother Shane sitting next to me in my truck, watching me shift gears, anxious for the time he could drive it.

"Hi," I said. "My name's Stony."

Logan blushed, grabbed his mom's arm, and turned his face away.

"He's a little bashful," Robyn said. "But that lasts only a few minutes."

I drove south out of the city, passing farms smelling of pigs, passing hundreds of acres of corn and soybeans on either side of the road.

I turned left onto a gravel road which narrowed into a dirt one, passed an abandoned farmhouse.

When we arrived at the park entrance, Robyn said, "It's beautiful here. And what an awesome September day."

"Wildcat Den," I said. "A county wilderness area hardly anyone knows about. Picnicking and hiking. Even swimming in the creek. Lots of deer, turkey, squirrel, rabbits. No hunting, though."

"What do you think, Logan?" she asked her three-year-old son as they jumped out of my truck. "Isn't this nice?"

A light breeze blew the treetops, swirling the colorful leaves.

"Potty, Mommy?" Logan said, dancing on his toes.

I pointed to a shelter fifty yards down the dirt path. "That way. Want me to take him?"

"I will."

"I'm a big boy," Logan said.

"Yes, you are," I agreed.

I settled at a picnic table in the shade of a tree-surrounded pavilion, watching Logan and Robyn trot off to the restroom. Wearing jean shorts and a white Mickey Mouse T-shirt, Logan held his mom's hand.

Who was his father?

Robyn wore black shorts. She was narrow-hipped. Her long, pale white legs flashed in the sunlight. She hadn't spent much time outdoors. She wore a long-sleeved black blouse, tight around the neck. Her floppy hat perched on her head.

When they returned, Logan climbed onto the picnic table, wiggled close to me, and said, "Are you my mommy's boyfriend?"

"Logan!" Robyn's face turned instant red.

I managed a little smile. "Your mommy's my teacher. She's going to make me smart like her. And you."

"I have an idea you're already smart," Robyn said. "You need to apply yourself."

"You sound like my counselor."

"Let's get started."

I tousled Logan's dark hair. "You going to help me, too?"

"I can spell my name. L-O-G-A-N." His eyes flashed proudly. "And I know my telephone number."

"Logan, shhh," Robyn said, silencing him, apparently not wanting him to give that secret away.

"That's great," I said. "I had a brother once. His name was Shane. He—" I halted abruptly. The fact that I even mentioned his name startled me. I left my thought hanging awkwardly in midair a moment, then said, "He's—he died."

Robyn looked at me. "What happened?"

"He tried to jump a southbound Soo Line freight. He grabbed one of the iron ladders on a boxcar, lost his grip."

"Oh, no . . ." Robyn said.

"The train was only going about ten miles per hour . . ."

My voice trailed off.

"That's terrible," Robyn said.

"I try not to think about it." I shrugged. "So, look, Logan, you never want to play on the railroad tracks. Okay, buddy?"

"I can play on swings," Logan said, pointing to the swings, slides, and monkey bars in a grassy playground off to the left.

"Good idea," Robyn said. "Wendell, you can copy my notes from the first unit—"

"Stony," I said.

"—and Logan and I'll play on the swings. When you're finished, I'll drill you on the lit terms Ms. Oberhaus likes to put on her tests."

"Sounds good. You want your money now?"

"Let's see how long this takes."

"All right."

I worked for nearly an hour copying Robyn's notes. Native Americans: Delaware, Navaho, Ojibwa. The Early Puritans: William Bradford, Ann Bradstreet, William Byrd, Jonathan Edwards. Boring stuff. Worse: Before I took the semester evaluation in January, I'd have to go back and read all the selections I'd ignored. *Damn.*

I worked another half hour memorizing lit terms.

I glanced up several times and watched Robyn pushing Logan high in the swing. Their laughter floated on the breeze. Soon Logan was zipping down the slide by himself. Later, while he played in the sand by the slide, Robyn was swinging herself high, kicking her legs, pumping on the chain, grinning. A little girl herself.

Then suddenly, I realized that the real reason she had grabbed the opportunity to help me today was that it meant she'd be able to take Logan to the park, getting him out into the air and sunshine. She didn't want the money. She'd used me.

That was all right. I could live with that.

When I finished, book and notebooks returned to my truck, I ambled over to the swing set. Robyn and Logan had swung themselves out. Robyn sat swaying back and forth in a swing, admiring the blue sky and flaming trees, while Logan played with two tiny cars in the dirt under one of the swings.

"Want to go for a hike?" I said.

Logan looked up. "Hike?"

"A walk through the woods. I'll guarantee we see deer."

"A lion, too?" Logan looked worried.

"No lion. Just a deer. Maybe more than one."

"How far do we have to walk?" Robyn said. "We don't exactly have hiking boots on."

I looked at their sandals. I should have told her to wear her combat boots.

"Not very far," I said. "The trail's wide and mostly flat. One hill. I'll carry Logan on my shoulders. You can quiz me about the lit terms. You need your notebook?"

"No." She thought a second. "Are there snakes?"

"I want to see a snake," Logan said.

"No snakes," I said.

"What about ticks?" Robyn said.

"We'll stay on the path," I assured her. "Don't be such a wimp."

After she wiped the dirt and sand off Logan's arms, legs, and bottom, I hoisted him to my shoulders and secured the boy by wrapping my arms around his feet. Robyn stuffed the tiny cars into the canvas bag and locked it in the truck.

Logan weighed no more than thirty pounds. Light as a feather. I could walk with him on my shoulders all day.

As we followed the path into the woods, I took the lead, Logan playfully thumping me on the head.

"Onomatopoeia?" Robyn said from behind me.

I wracked my brain for a second, then frowned. "Start with something easy."

"I thought you studied these."

"I did. Ask me something else."

Originally a deer trail, the path twisted through the woods of tall oak, hickory, and ash. Tree branches formed a tunnel of colorful leaves over it, creating shade, keeping the air cool, while a breeze rustled the treetops.

Robyn explained onomatopoeia, then said, "Analogy?"

I nodded my head confidently. "An analogy," I said, "explains something unfamiliar by comparing it to something familiar."

"Right. Allusion?"

"A short reference to a person, place, event, or another work of literature that the writer expects the reader to recognize."

"Very good. Aphorism?"

"A statement expressing a wise or clever observation about life. Like, 'No pain no gain.'"

"Nice."

She must have thrown fifteen terms like that at me as we hiked through the woods—I got them nearly all right—when I halted suddenly on the path.

She bumped into me from behind.

"What's wrong?" she said.

I eased off to the side of the path. "Shhh . . . don't move."

Thirty yards ahead of us, off the trail in a clearing in the woods, stood a doe and its dappled fawn. The doe was motionless, staring at us. The fawn foraged on the ground, unaware it was being watched.

"Deers!" Logan squealed, and yanked at my pigtail, jarring my head back.

"Ouch!"

At the sound of our voices, the doe tilted her head, ears erect, and gathered our scent with her quivering nose. Suddenly she whirled and bounded deep into the woods, her white tail bobbing, and the fawn scrambled to follow its mother.

"I told you!" I said.

"Cool!" Robyn said. "I've never seen a deer in the wild before."

"He jumped and ran away," Logan said, clapping his hands over my head.

After that, the path wound up a steep hill, then down. I took Robyn's hand, making sure she didn't slip and fall. Suddenly, I wondered what she was doing tonight. Would she like to go out? What would she like to do? What would I tell Mindy?

Don't even think about it, Stony!

eight

On the way home, as soon as I turned my truck from the Wildcat Den gravel road onto the county blacktop, Logan fell asleep.

"He usually doesn't get worn out so soon," Robyn said.

"Good country air," I told her.

Logan lay snuggled in his car seat, his head cranked toward Robyn. He didn't look comfortable, but he was sleeping anyway.

"Thanks for your help today," I said. "I owe you at least forty-five dollars."

"We'll talk about it later."

While she hugged her door, I studied her and said, "Explain to me, why are you tutoring?"

She flipped her hair behind her ears. "Five or six of us are. I don't know about the others, but someday . . . I want to make a difference in the world. This is a start."

I was thinking that by helping me she was getting a pretty slow start. And what kind of goal was that, anyway? I mean, how could she make a difference, one slender girl by herself?

"You'd like to be a teacher?" I said.

"Journalism, I think. Psychology—I don't know. What about you? What are your plans? Go to college? Play football?"

I fanned my fingers out on the steering wheel. "My dad has always worked in the quarry. My grandpa did, too. That's what I planned to do, but lately . . . I don't know, either."

"You like living here?"

"Love it. Love living in Hickory Ridge. Love the hunting and fishing. Love the river."

"Nothing wrong with that."

"But my counselor, Mr. Duval, says there's another life out there for me if I want it, but I have to turn my grades around. Set some goals. Make some smart choices."

"Good advice. And your first goal is to pass your American Lit test on Monday."

"If I do, you get the credit."

"Not me. You're doing the work." Then she said, "I read about last night's game in the paper this morning. Things didn't go very well, did they?"

"None of us were ready to play. Not without Brian."

I felt her eyes on me.

"You don't seem like a football player."

That brought a faint smile. "What's a football player supposed to be like? Aren't I big, ugly, and mean enough?"

"It's just that I've read things about you in the paper. 'Vicious hit.' 'Bone-jarring tackle.' I read that you 'deck' players. 'Flatten' them."

"When you 'pancake' them, that's the best."

"It all seems so violent—I hate violence. But you don't seem like that at all—I watched you with Logan."

"I like little kids," I admitted. "I liked my brother a lot. We were buddies. I miss him."

I was thinking maybe if I just told her what happened to Shane, and explained my part in it, I wouldn't think about it anymore. Today, at least. I'd never talked about Shane's death with anybody except Mindy and Brain, and though everybody in town knew what had happened, only my girlfriend and my buddy understood how guilty I felt—I think my folks might have suspected.

Robyn said, "You want to talk about it."

I shot her a glance. It was like she was reading my mind. I adjusted the rearview mirror—it didn't need adjusting.

I stared ahead at the road a minute.

"The thing is, Shane had seen me jump boxcars and coal cars hundreds of times. I'm four years older than him. He always wanted to do everything I did." I stopped to swallow a lump in my throat.

"That's understandable."

"See, to jump a boxcar you have to be running faster than the train's going because when you, like, jump, the train's pulling in front a little while you're in the air. Besides that, the boxcars sway back and forth."

"That's too dangerous to even think about doing."

"And you have to time your jump so the ladder rung is swaying toward you."

"Is that possible?"

"Sure. And you have to grab a rung on the ladder and anchor your feet on the lowest rung practically at the same time. If you don't anchor your feet, you're left hanging there, bouncing against the car."

I stopped again. My eyes were starting to burn. I peered out the windshield at the wild sunflowers blowing in the ditch, their yellow heads bobbing.

"Shane didn't run fast enough," I said. "Didn't time his jump. Didn't anchor his feet."

"You saw it?"

"He was with his friends. They told me." Suddenly I felt as if I was sweating. "It was his first jump. He wasn't very coordinated. Wasn't good at sports, but he always wanted to be like me."

"If you're blaming yourself, you shouldn't be."

"He wanted to do everything I did. He wouldn't have tried it if he hadn't seen me do it. It was *all* my fault."

"That's not necessarily true."

I felt myself gripping the steering wheel harder.

"And since his death my mom and dad fight all the time. They drink. I try not to let any of it bother me—but *shit!*"

I glanced at her again. That was it. That was enough. I was getting worked up, my throat aching like it always does at times like this. I didn't want to talk about Shane any longer. I took deep breaths, letting them out long and slow. *Fuck!* I was almost falling apart in front of her.

Finally, my breathing leveled out, my fingers relaxed on the steering wheel, and I said, "Look, how about if you tell me something about yourself?"

"Like what?"

"Are you an athlete?"

"A gymnast. Fifth, sixth, seventh grades. Uneven and parallel bars were my best events."

"Any good?"

"Yes. I loved it. Especially the parallel bars."

"So why'd you stop?"

She shrugged. "Things happen. I lost interest."

"But you loved it."

Silence. I expected her to say more, but when she didn't, I said, "Where do you come from?"

"Wethersfield, Connecticut. It's by Hartford. I came to school here during the middle of last year."

"Your parents got money. Right?"

"How do you know?"

"Something about the way you walk. Talk."

"You think I'm a snob?"

"If you were, you wouldn't be helping me. Why are you living with your sister?"

"Take a guess."

I pursed my lips, giving the matter some thought. "You got pregnant. Your folks didn't like the guy and got mad because you decided to keep the baby. They threw both of you out."

I wished I hadn't said all that. It sounded cold.

"Close enough," she said.

"Go out with me tonight?" The words leaped out of my mouth before I could stop them. But the moment I heard them, I knew I'd made a killer mistake.

If by some miracle Robyn said yes, I'd be in deep, deep trouble. Saturday night was Alicia's party. Mindy had been opening early on Saturday mornings at McDonald's so she could be off by five, and later we could party every Saturday night.

After leaving her last night at the Romp, ditching her tonight would be like playing in a roaring bonfire.

"You're crazy," Robyn said.

"Lots of parties on Saturday night."

She said, "For one thing, I don't party. For another, I don't date."

"Life must be boring."

"You already have a girlfriend. Every girl in school knows about you and Mindy."

"She doesn't have a rope around my neck."

"She writes about you in the girls' restroom as if she does."

I blinked. Laughed a little. But it wasn't a funny laugh. "Writes about me?"

Robyn nodded.

"I don't believe it."

"I've seen her leaving the stall," Robyn said. "Felt pen in hand."

"Writes about what?"

"What a stud you are. How you make her feel."

Now I was frowning. "You're kidding."

"Why would I kid you? Check it out. Second floor. Girls' restroom at the northeast corner of the building. Third stall from the entrance."

I still didn't believe it. Writing on the walls of a restroom stall, that's what guys do. Not girls. Or do they? The second floor restroom, though, northeast corner, was where Mindy always grabbed a cigarette before she met me by my locker before fourth period. She liked to talk dirty over the phone. Why not write dirty on restroom walls?

If it was true, I needed to have a word with Mindy.

Logan squirmed and mumbled, "Deers run away . . ." As he snuggled deeper into his car seat, he slipped his thumb into his mouth.

When I pulled my truck to a halt in front of Robyn's sister's house, I said, "You sure you won't change your mind?"

I knew she wouldn't, but I didn't see any harm in keeping pressure on her. Maybe if I ever became available, I'd ask her out again.

She shook her head and gave me an emphatic, "No, thank you." But her voice softened a little as she said, "But thanks for putting up with Logan and me, taking us to the park."

"My pleasure, believe me."

"I'm sure he had a good time. I hope you do well on your test. Review your lit terms again. Check out onomatopoeia."

I thumped a finger off my forehead. "Onomatopoeia: the use of words with sounds that suggest their meaning. Like *crrrack!* A branch breaking."

"Very good."

"Maybe we can do something together again," I said. "All three of us." Another brilliant idea hit me. "I'll take you fishing—has Logan ever gone fishing? They really hit this time of year."

"We can't." She gathered Logan into her arms.

"Why not? How about some Saturday or Sunday morning?"

Hopping out of the truck, I hurried around and opened the door for her. I'd never done that for Mindy.

"I'll bet Logan would like fishing," I said.

"No," she said firmly. "You and I are not dating. We're not going fishing."

I unbuckled the car seat and grabbed the bag of toys for her.

Clutching Logan against her chest in her left arm, she snatched the car seat and bag of toys from me with her right hand, stepped around me, then strode across the walk up to her sister's house.

"Robyn—"

"NO!" She didn't look back.

I shook my head. I usually didn't fail that miserably with girls. But since committing to Mindy, I really hadn't tried to hit on anyone. Maybe it wasn't me. Maybe it was what Mindy was writing about me in the girls' restroom.

It wasn't until I was halfway home that I realized I hadn't paid Robyn the forty-five dollars I owed her. Maybe more than that.

nine

When I bounded into the house at four in the afternoon, the place was empty, the phone ringing. My ribs still hurt a little.

Had to be Mindy.

I hadn't talked to her since ditching her last night at the bonfire.

Like I said, she opened early on Saturdays at McDonald's, and I hoped she didn't drink too much last night. I always kept an eye on her. Tried to slow her down. I hoped she stayed out of trouble and got to work on time.

I let the phone ring and ring and ring.

No one else would be as persistent as Mindy.

Sitting at the dirty dish-cluttered kitchen table, I drank a half quart of milk and ate two stale donuts. I rummaged through the refrigerator for something else to eat. Nothing but leftover pizza with furry green mold on top, a spoiled baked potato turning black, and a chicken leg someone had taken a bite out of. Probably me.

The phone was still ringing.

In the freezer on top of the fridge, I found a ring of bologna. I zapped it in the microwave to thaw it a bit, then dumped it into a saucepan of water to bring it to a boil.

Still the phone was ringing.

A few days ago my life was okay. Nothing spectacular. But moving along okay. Then my F in American Lit popped up and the problem of staying eligible to play football. Then Duval threw this question at me again. *What are you going to do with the rest of your life?*

Now Mindy was getting on my nerves more than ever. And Brian, my friend, the best quarterback in the state, was bleeding internally. Out of action. Maybe his life in danger, I didn't know.

Then there was Robyn. Brainy but mysterious Robyn Knight, my tutor, with a neat little kid named Logan, who kept reminding me of Shane.

Rrring! Rrring! Rrring!

Onomatopoeia!

My life had suddenly gotten complicated, and I was heating bologna in a pan of water, worried about what the hell I should do. What *is* this? *I'm worried!*

As the phone continued to ring, I grabbed the cordless and sat again at the kitchen table. When the ringing stopped, I called Brian's house, hoping to find out from his mom or dad how he was doing.

His mom answered and recognized my voice immediately.

"Oh, Stony," she said. "How are you?"

"How's Brian? That's the question."

"They've stopped the bleeding. He's recovering. He'll be home Monday." Her voice sounded flat. "He could have died."

"What caused it?"

A moment's silence. "You don't really know, do you?"

I wanted to say, *Maybe.*

"No, I don't," I said. "Not for sure."

"He's been taking over-the-counter painkillers, I don't know for how long. They ate a hole in the lining of his stomach."

My jaw dropped to the table. "Ate a hole? You're kidding."

"A lot of those pills you've got to take with food. He never did that."

"I can't believe it. A hole?"

"And why he was taking all those pills he doesn't want to say. They're not the kind kids are getting high on, are they?"

"I don't think so."

"Do you have any idea why he was taking them?"

I closed my eyes.

I didn't know what to say. Like I said, I didn't want to rat Brian out. But I wanted the best for him. Was this something like, *Friends don't let friends drive drunk*? Analogy.

"His dad thinks it's his arm," Mrs. Hall said. "His elbow, actually."

That's all I needed. "It is his elbow," I said. "It's been hurting in practice and in games. He didn't want to tell the coach. Didn't want to get benched."

"Oh, Lord . . ." Then, in a voice that seemed to scold me, "How long have you known this, Stony."

"Not very long. Just the other day, really. Brian and I haven't been hanging together as much."

During a long silence, I heard her blow her nose, the tissue brushing the phone.

Finally she said, "Well, it's not your fault, anyway. I don't know what got into that boy, thinking he could get away with something like taking pills."

"That wasn't very smart," I said.

"Thank you for saying something."

I knew damn well Brian wouldn't thank me.

Then we talked briefly about last night's game and how sad it was that we lost. She didn't know when Brian would be back out for football. At last she said, "Come see him Monday after practice. He's feeling really low."

"I will, Mrs. Hall. I promise."

As soon as I placed the receiver back in its cradle on the wall, the phone rang. This time I lifted it off the hook.

"Hello?"

"W-where the hell have you been?" Mindy sputtered. "I've been calling all day. Even from work. No answer. Now your line's busy."

"Have fun last night?"

"Not without you."

I didn't know if I believed her or not. Once early in our relationship, she cheated on me with an old boyfriend. She said it was my fault because I hadn't committed to her yet, and she was free to do whatever she wanted. I'd let the incident go but hadn't forgotten it.

"I could not *believe* you left without me," she said.

"How'd you get home?"

"Dale and Sheila. I was late for work this morning. Got chewed out. Happens again they might fire me. I don't care—I hate that job. Who were you talking to?"

"Brian's mom. He'll be okay. He'll be home Monday."

"Good. Maybe the team will get its ass in gear, and you won't have to take the blame for everything."

"I'm not taking the blame."

I decided not to tell her the details about Brian's hospital stay. She'd blab it all over school. I'm sure he didn't want that.

"Where have you been?"

"Studying for my American Lit test."

"All afternoon? I've been calling and calling your house."

"I went to a park where it was quiet. This phone doesn't ring there."

"What park?"

"Wildcat Den."

A moment's silence.

"Were you alone, Stony?"

"Why are you asking these questions?"

"Why won't you answer me?"

I hesitated.

Then Mindy said, "You were with *her*, weren't you? Your tutor bitch!"

"I needed her help."

"You took her to *our* park?"

"It's not *our* park!"

"It's where we screwed the first time. Or don't you remember? What's going on, Stony?"

"Nothing!"

"This isn't you! You're doing stuff you've never done before. Library seventh period, study. Home Friday night, sleep. Wildcat Den Saturday afternoon, study with your geeky tutor."

"I have to."

"She's got a giant dragon tattooed on her back—Deb saw it Friday in the shower after PE."

"That's a lie! You're saying that shit—she's a druggie, she's got needle tracks on her arm, tattoos on her back—so I'll dump her as a tutor."

"Why don't you believe me anymore?"

"She's too smart for any of that weird stuff. She's got too much class."

"Talk to me, Stony. Tell me what's happening."

My neck felt warm. I was getting irritated.

I said, "I don't know what's happening, all right? There's so much shit going on, I'm trying to deal with it, but I don't know what to do."

"I tried to help you out last night, but you wouldn't let me."

Then I let fly with, "You are *not* what I need."

The silence was deafening. Finally, I heard Mindy suck in a deep breath. "What the hell does that mean?"

I bowed my head and rubbed my neck. I shouldn't have said that. "I didn't mean it the way it sounded. I didn't mean anything."

"I heard you say I am *not* what you need."

"Mindy—"

She slammed the receiver down, leaving my ears ringing.

I hung up the phone, and closed my eyes. I felt awful. Mindy didn't deserve that. Shane died two years ago. He was twelve. I was sixteen. That's about the time Mindy and I first hooked up. I spent hours at Wildcat Den with her in my arms in the bed of my pickup truck, wrapped in a sleeping bag. She let me drown myself in her flesh, never holding back. She was what I needed then, a way to escape. She wasn't what I needed now, though. And I didn't understand. *Jesus!*

I speared the ring of bologna with a fork, lifted it out of the boiling water, and set it on a paper plate. Bread. Right now I needed bread. I found three slices of Wonder Bread in a wrapper in the bread box. One slice was the heel. Tiny specks of blue mold grew on the crust of each slice, but I cut them off.

Any old cheese? I could always cut the mold off cheese, too.

The phone rang.

I closed my eyes again, listening to its rattling sound.

Had to be Mindy.

I answered on the sixth ring. "Hello?"

"I'm sorry." Mindy was crying. I could hardly make out her words between her sobs. "I love you, Stony."

Possessive, jealous, and short-tempered as she was, I couldn't imagine anyone else as loving and passionate as Mindy.

And impulsive. One time at school, she dragged me into the custodians' closet to perform her before-game favor.

"None of it's your fault," I said. "It's me, I'm all screwed up."

"It's *all* my fault," she said, sniffling. "I know how much football means to you—Brian, too—and I know you've got to win now more than ever, and I know you could never fall for a skinny mud duck like Robyn Knight. It's just—I love you so much, Stony. I don't think I could live without you. Do you love me?"

"Mindy, c'mon . . ."

"Say it, Stony. Say you love me."

I licked my lips and said, "I love you, Mindy, babe."

She kissed me over the phone. *Smack!* "I'll always love you. After we graduate and get married, we won't fight like this."

"Mindy, please . . ."

"Pick me up tonight?"

"Sure."

We made arrangements and when I hung up, for the first time in my life, I felt trapped. Not just by Mindy but by everything that was going on. I mean, I felt like I was floundering in a maze, and I couldn't grope my way out.

For sure, I couldn't find anything to smile about.

Then I remembered I hadn't asked Mindy about her writing on the restroom walls at school. Hadn't I promised myself to have a word with her about that?

And I still owed Robyn forty-five dollars. At least.

ten

"Remember Alicia's party from last year?" Mindy said, when I picked her up in front of her house. "How can I forget?" I said.

It was eight o'clock. Darkness had settled over Thompsonville. The sky was clear with a million bright stars hanging out, waiting for the moon to show.

The chilly night air hopped into the truck with Mindy. She left the door ajar so the dome light would stay on.

Mindy said, "That stupid Ralph Hudson got lost in the cornfield. I wonder if he'll be there tonight."

"He walked in a few rows to take a leak and couldn't find his way out. I couldn't believe it."

Ralph was a third-string defensive back on our team, not too bright, always doing stupid things. Like one time at a party he fell into the bonfire. But it had been raining, and his clothes were soaked, so he didn't get burned bad at all.

Mindy said, "Do I look all right?" The tip of her tongue glided around her red lips, leaving them wet and shiny.

Low-slung jeans with a black leather belt and a big silver buckle hugged her butt. She also wore a blue half T-shirt and a light-blue jacket, unzipped so you could see her pierced belly button.

A braided ponytail pulled back her rusty-brown hair, emphasizing her oval face with her wide-set eyes, highlighted tonight with dark eye shadow and mascara. Gold earrings dangled from her lobes.

"How do I look?" she repeated. She liked compliments about her appearance.

"Fine."

"Is that all you can say?"

When I didn't reply, she closed the door and slid next to me, her hand on my thigh. She kissed me on the cheek—my lip was still sore—and her scent made my nose itch.

She said, "Alicia's parents are in Chicago again. I think the party's going to be in the garage, like last time. We'll have a blast." She squeezed my leg. "What's wrong?"

I scratched my nose. "You're writing stuff about us on the restroom walls at school, aren't you?"

Her hand twitched on my thigh.

"Who said I was?"

"Are you?"

"Who said?"

"Answer the question!"

Mindy let out a long hiss of exasperation. "Robyn Knight said I did, didn't she? She eyed me coming out of a stall the other day. She probably stuck her head in there. Nosy bitch."

"What kind of stuff are you writing?"

"Nothing! Nothing bad—just stuff."

I stared at her. "What—*stuff?*"

"What we do. How it feels to get off like that. Custodians always scrub it away—I think the bitches like to read it."

"Guys write on restroom walls," I said. "Scumballs! Not girls."

"You're calling me a scumball?"

"I'm telling you to knock it off!"

"I don't use our names."

"I don't care! Knock it off!"

• • •

When we got to Alicia's party, flashy new cars and pickups lined both sides of the gravel lane leading up to the farmhouse, where Alicia lived with her mom and dad. The way

I got it was Alicia's folks were rich. They owned this thousand-acre farm, and her mom liked to go on weekend shopping sprees in Chicago, 180 miles away. Her dad was more than willing to leave Alicia home alone. By leaving his daughter behind, he figured he cut his shopping bill in half. If not more.

When he did that, though, Alicia threw parties. She used the huge unattached three-car garage—almost an airplane hanger—next to the house, lugging out a Ping Pong table, dart board, boombox, and card tables from the rec room in the house, setting up the gear in the garage, parking her mom's car outside. Girls could use the restroom in the house. Guys went outside at their favorite bush, tree, or fence post.

By the time Mindy and I arrived, we weren't talking to each other. Silently, we climbed out of my truck and stood under the glow of a yard light perched on top of a telephone pole. A German shepherd ambled over to us, tail wagging, whining deep in his throat, begging to be petted. This is the dog that found Ralph in the cornfield last year when three other guys and I were searching for him. I bent down and scratched his ears. "How you doing, Buddy?"

Because I was paying more attention to the dog than to her, Mindy threw her chin out and huffed off for the garage. The garage's windowless double-wide door was down, the service door closed, a sheet probably covering the two side windows. The idea was to keep all the laughter, music, beer, and drunken kids inside. But even so, as I patted the dog's side, I swear I could feel the music's bass pulsing through the air, and I caught the fragrant scent of pigs. In this state, farmers call it the smell of money.

I didn't stop Mindy from going ahead. She could get lost in the crowd, have a few beers, settle down. Her writing graffiti like that really bothered me. That and her drinking and smoking. And her being so possessive. And lately her hinting about marriage.

When I stepped inside the garage and closed the service door behind me, the party was going full blast.

Loud chatter, laughter, and music bounced off the garage's well-insulated, paneled walls, making it almost impossible to hear.

Cigarette and marijuana smoke hung so thick in the air my eyes stung. At the far end of the garage, ten kids, maybe, were playing cards at two different card tables under a fluorescent light hanging from the ceiling.

Up front, where I was standing, kids were crushed together in the dark, dancing. A joint floated into my hand. I passed it up and headed for the Ping Pong table where there was food. But before I got there, Alicia materialized, frowning up at me.

"Mindy's someplace around here. Are you guys fighting tonight?"

A blond, Alicia was built like Mindy—not quite as good—a bit taller, and just as horny. And she was a player. Different stud every weekend. Mindy and she were best buddies in junior high, but when I latched on to Mindy in senior high, they drifted apart. They didn't have time for each other.

"Why the fight?" Alicia said.

"Nothing to worry about."

"I got the answer. Hayloft. Do it in the hayloft. I've lived on this farm seventeen years and did it in the hayloft last week for the first time. It's a blast."

"No doubt."

"You ever been tickled nearly to death with a strand of hay? Tickled everywhere?"

Before I could say no and turn down Alicia's generous offer, I felt someone slipping a cold can of beer into my hand.

Good old reliable Mindy.

"Thanks," I mumbled.

I popped the can, cleared my throat, and sipped. By that time Alicia had slithered away.

"What did she want?" Mindy said.

"She was offering us her hayloft."

"Cool."

Mindy finished her beer with a chug and set the empty on the corner of the Ping Pong table. I took only a sip of mine.

She pulled my head down so she could whisper in my ear. "You know why I write in the restroom?"

"Why?"

"Because I'm proud of what we have. Of you and me. I want every girl in school to read it and be jealous. Wish she was me." She kissed my ear. "That's why I write it."

Mindy stretched on her tiptoes, and her mouth reached mine for a soft kiss that didn't bother my lip.

"I don't know why we're fighting so much lately, Stony. All I want to do is please you. I'm so jealous. I know I am. I can't help it—I love you. I can't wait till we're married and you're really mine."

I flinched. I felt a sudden intense pressure, like an entire offensive line was trying to flatten me.

"Maybe sex isn't enough," I said, surprising myself. I stepped back, thinking I should duck. I mean, like, the idea had come from out of nowhere, but having said it, I knew it was true.

Mindy's eyes got wide, and her dark eyebrows bunched.

"What did you say?"

I shrugged.

"T-there has to be something else," stumbled out of my mouth.

"You think someone else can do you better?"

"I didn't say that."

"I do everything for you, I do it all."

"That's not what I'm saying."

Her look was poison. "What! What *are* you saying?"

Before she could really unload on me, Alicia swung by and grabbed Mindy's arm. "Got something for you," Alicia said to Mindy.

"What?" Mindy spoke to Alicia, but Mindy's eyes, all smoke and fire, were riveted on me.

"You'll see." Alicia tugged at Mindy's arm, and they sailed off into the crowd, Alicia calling over her shoulder, "We'll be right back."

Right.

I ate a plate full of chips, dip, cheese, salami. I finished off my beer and headed for the card tables. That was where the beer was last year, iced in a tub in a corner.

I mingled on the way. Shot the breeze with a couple of guys from our team, mostly about Brian. Ted Jacobs, offensive lineman, said, "Something like what happened to Brian happened to my mom. Ulcer ate a hole in the lining of her stomach size of a quarter. Took a long time to heal. Lots of things she couldn't eat."

"Brian's tough," I said. "He'll be okay."

I nodded hello to a couple of girls. I wondered if Robyn would like a party like this. Probably not.

There were two guys playing blackjack at a table of six I'd never seen before. The sight of them sent a shiver down my spine. Each sported a shaved head, and a diamond stud in a gold setting flashed in each one's left earlobe. Each wore black jeans and a red T-shirt. Tilted to the left, a black-and-red ball cap perched on each one's head.

Who invited these guys?

I didn't remember seeing them around our school.

I sensed trouble. This was no place for me. Especially if a fight broke out, the cops arrived, and we were all hauled off to jail. I didn't need that—I was having enough trouble staying eligible for football.

"Who you staring at?" When the thin one with a pimply face spoke to me, his right eye twitched.

"Watching the game, bro," I said easily, and found a crooked smile for him.

The bigger, muscular one raised his dark eyes. "Never seen guys play blackjack before?"

"You should've stayed with seventeen," I said. "Taking a hit at that point gets you busted three times out of five." I didn't know if that was true or not. I just couldn't resist pulling his chain.

But that wasn't smart.

Both straightened, scowling.

Muscles said, "Me and Frank don't like no disrespect." He sported a dark beard and mustache.

"No disrespect intended," I said politely.

At that moment Ralph Hudson tottered up to me, clutching a beer, eyes glassy, his smile lopsided. "Hey, Stony, dude! What's happening?"

I said, "Be cool, man."

But for some unknown reason, Ralph lurched—I don't think anyone pushed him—and spilled beer on Pimple Face. "Hey! Jesus Christ!" he yelled.

Ralph staggered back, mumbling, "Sorry."

"So what! I'm soaked!"

"He didn't mean it," I said, and grabbed Ralph by the shoulder. "I'll take care of him."

"What about my shirt?"

I didn't answer. I dragged Ralph through the crowd, looking back to see if we were being followed. We weren't.

Ralph kept asking, "What's happening? What's happening, man?"

At the front of the garage, I opened the service door and tossed Ralph into the chilly night. "Stay out there a while! Sober up, but keep out of the cornfield. I'll take you home in a minute."

"What's happening . . . ?"

I slammed the door in his face.

Suddenly the garage felt hot, its smoky air burning my eyes, nose, throat, lungs.

The music throbbed in my ears.

I spotted Mindy and Alicia by the Ping Pong table. I elbowed my way through the crowd toward them. When Alicia saw me, she vanished. A can of beer in her hand, Mindy appeared wobbly.

"How many you had?" I said, taking her can from her, setting it on the table. "Where you been?" I wished I could see her eyes in this dimness.

"In the house."

"Alicia give you something? What are you on?"

"Nothin', baby." She grinned. "Alicia tell you about her hayloft? Let's fuck."

"You're shitfaced already!" Guiding her by the elbow, I backed her into a corner. "We're out of here."

Mindy answered with a kiss, her body crushed against me. "Let's go."

"Not the hayloft. I mean we're leaving this party. Couple of guys here that don't belong."

Someone stumbled into my back, elbowing me.

My head jerked around. I thought it was one of the bald ones.

"Sorry, man," a guy with a cigarette dangling from his mouth said. "Someone pushed me. Sorry, man."

I gave him a look and turned back to Mindy.

She said, "People come and go at these parties. They won't stay long." She grabbed both my hands. "Let's go. Hayloft."

I took a breath and nearly choked on the smoke. "We're leaving."

Her head cocked, her shadowed eyes on me, she said, "I'm staying. I'm sleeping over so I can help Alicia drag all this stuff back into the house in the morning. You can sleep over, too, and help."

"I can't. I promised my mom I'd work for her tomorrow. I have to open the bait shop at six. Let's go."

I pulled her by the hand, but she yanked it away, stumbling back against the wall.

"I'm not leaving!" She spit the words at me. "Sex isn't enough—what's that mean *exactly?*"

"Didn't you hear what I said?" I waved a hand. "We're out of here. And I have to take Ralph home."

"I'm not leaving," she said again. "You did this to me last night." Her chin jutted. "But not tonight. If you walk out on me tonight—"

"What? What'll happen?"

"All I've ever done is try to please you and you treat me like shit!" She stabbed my chest with a finger. "*Asshole! Prick! Fucker!*" She rattled off names as if she was calling roll in a classroom.

"Mindy—"

"Go!" she screamed, and beat on my chest with her fists. "Get the fuck out of here!"

I spun on my heels. I elbowed, nudged, and bulled my way through the crowd, ripped open the door, and plunged into the night, leaving the shiny faces, shrill laughter, and pounding music behind me.

Outside, I stood in the grass and tossed my head back. I hoped to breathe in fresh air, but I inhaled the scent of pigs and nearly gagged. At least a full moon had come out to party with the stars.

I looked at my watch. Eleven o'clock. I couldn't remember the last Saturday night I'd been home before midnight.

I scouted around in the moonlight for Ralph. I circled the garage and found a couple in back, grappling and moaning against the building. They apparently didn't know about the hayloft.

No Ralph. No Buddy, either. Alicia must have locked the dog in the house.

If Ralph went back into that party, one of those black-jack-playing bald apes might kill him. I hoped he wasn't staggering around in the cornfield again. I finally gave up.

I climbed into my truck, wondering what Robyn was doing tonight. It was too late to find out.

I thought, *I'll call her tomorrow from the bait shop.*

That was out. I didn't know her telephone number. I should have asked Logan. He would have told me.

eleven

The next morning, I rolled out of bed at 5:30 AM, feeling alive. Imagine. When was the last time I felt this good on a Sunday morning? When I drove to the all-night Quick Stop on the highway, the morning was dark and chilly. The moon had deserted, and only a few stars lingered.

From fat old lady Lyons, the all-night clerk at the Quick Stop, I bought a quart of milk, a dozen donuts, and a newspaper. I bought the paper because I wanted to check out Saturday night's football scores.

I opened the bait shop at six. Right on time. Dawn was creeping in. I pulled the chain on all three fluorescent ceiling lights, lighting the shop brightly.

Two middle-aged fisherman dressed in striped bibs and wearing straw hats walked in at 6:02, wanting two dozen crappie minnows in each of their buckets.

Business was brisk all morning.

But between customers, I kept wondering about Mindy.

I felt guilty having left her at Alicia's party. I probably shouldn't have done that. I couldn't imagine what kind of trouble she might have gotten into. When I left, she was pretty wasted.

How would she get home this morning?

Was this the end between us?

The bell suddenly tinkled above the door, and I was ready for another group of fishermen wanting bait and advice. But it was Mom who stood in the doorway at eight o'clock, looking pale, frightened, and angry.

"I can't believe it!" Mom ran her fingers through her gray-streaked dark hair.

"What is it?" I said.

The only thing I could think of was that Dad had been picked up a third time for drunk driving. Though he eventually got his driver's license back after the first two times, a third offense could mean jail time.

Mom said, "If your friends have done this I want them to stop."

"Dad's all right?"

"He's just getting up." Mom's lips turned thin. "I want to know who did this. It's got to come off."

"What?" I said.

"Spray painted our house!" Mom's eyes flashed. "A giant red heart. And I want it washed off right now! I don't want the neighbors to see."

I felt my mouth fall open. "Our house?"

"Go look! Tell me who did it."

"How do I know?"

"What are kids thinking of these days? I want that off the house right now!"

Two fishermen straggled in, getting a late start. They looked hung over.

Mom forced a smile and said, "What can I do for you, boys?" She stepped behind the counter. "Go home," Mom said to me. "I'll take care of the shop. You take care of what I told you."

"It probably won't wash off."

"I want it off! Now!"

• • •

I stood on the sidewalk and stared at the graffiti spray painted on the east side of our corner house, the side that faced the street. Rising above the trees, the sun hit the art-work like a spotlight. Anyone driving by could see the artist's masterpiece perfectly.

Dad stood beside me, drinking his Sunday morning cocktail from an eighteen-ounce plastic cup: beer and tomato juice poured over ice with a touch of Tabasco sauce. Just a little salt and pepper.

Dad shook his head. "It doesn't mean nothing. Just kids. Hell, I spray painted things when I was a kid, too."

"Outhouses," I said. "Not someone's house."

"I wonder what it's supposed to mean?" Dad said.

I studied the red heart, maybe two feet tall, a foot and a half wide, three drops of blood dripping from the bottom.

I said, "It's nothing I've ever seen before. Doesn't look like a gang symbol. Mom wants me to get it off the house."

"Scrape it with a putty knife," Dad said. "Lot of it'll come off with the loose paint. Then paint over it. Got some house paint in the basement."

"You mean paint the whole side of the house," I said.

Dad sipped his cocktail. "Hell, no. Just over that heart. Might paint the house this fall, anyway."

Later, as I scraped and painted, I wondered why my house had been selected. I mean, like, nobody's house in Hickory Ridge has ever been spray painted. Why *my* house?

Must have been Mindy.

Was she so pissed at me for leaving her at a party for the second night in a row that she talked Alicia into giving her a ride here to spray paint my house? She was drunk enough to do something like that. She wrote on restroom walls. Why not spray paint my house?

The drops of blood were her tears. *Symbols.*

I slapped more paint on the side of our house with my paint brush, covering the last of the blood-dripping heart.

I needed to have a serious talk with Alicia and Mindy.

twelve

I spotted two guys leaving Alicia's house when I arrived at ten in the morning and eased my pickup into a crawl along the gravel road in front of her farmhouse.

I watched them skylark across the yard, punching each other on the shoulder and laughing as they piled into a red Mustang. Buddy, the German shepherd, bolted from the barn and barked at them. The Mustang driver wheeled the little car around, tried to hit the dog, then headed out of the yard and zoomed down the gravel lane, leaving a dusty wake in front of me.

I didn't recognize them, but it wasn't hard to guess what was going on. They'd slept here last night.

Slept with Alicia and Mindy.

I pulled my truck into the yard, climbed out, and headed for the side door of the house, where the two guys had just exited. Buddy trotted along beside me, wagging his tail, sniffing my jeans.

I pulled open the storm door and tried the knob on the solid wood door behind it. It was locked.

I beat on the wooden door.

"What?" Alicia screamed from inside. She probably thought I was one of those guys returning.

"Let me in!" I yelled, and twisted the knob. "I want to talk to Mindy."

"Go away!" Mindy yelled back.

"No!"

"Get lost, Stony!" Alicia was yelling at me this time.

"I'll break the door down. Explain that to your parents."

A moment's silence followed, except for Buddy barking behind me.

Locks snapped and clicked. The door inched open, secured by a safety chain.

"Go away!" Mindy said, peeping at me with one dark, baggy eye.

Questions leaped out of my mouth. "What's going on? What happened here last night? Who were those guys just leaving?"

"None of your business," Mindy said.

"Are you all right?"

"What the hell do you care?"

"Let me in or I'll bust that chain right out of the woodwork."

I heard them whispering frantically.

Suddenly the door closed, the chain clanked against the door, and then the door opened slowly, the two girls standing in the doorway, blocking me.

My mouth dropped.

Mindy and Alicia looked as if they'd been dragged across the yard behind a truck—clothes rumpled and dirty, hair tangled, faces smudged. Eyes red like they'd been crying.

Alicia looked worse because her left eye was red and swollen, nearly closed, and turning black.

"What happened?" I said. "You guys all right?"

"What's it look like?" Alicia said.

"If you'd have stayed last night," Mindy said, "none of this would've happened."

I stared at Alicia. I couldn't believe how bad she looked. Was that bits of straw I saw in her blond hair? "Did one of those guys belt you?" I asked her. "Or did you fall out of the hayloft?"

"Fuck you!" Alicia fired back.

"Stony, shut up!" From Mindy.

"You going to let me in? Or do I have to stand outside all day?"

Both girls turned and trudged up two steps into the kitchen. I followed them, closing the doors behind me, and smelled bacon and coffee.

The girls plunked down at the kitchen table, which was littered with dirty plates, silverware, and coffee cups for two. Toast crumbs, an open butter tub, jar of jelly, and three or four crumbled napkins also cluttered the table.

I leaned against the sink and crossed my arms.

"Those guys," I said, "stayed all night. One of them gives you a black eye, Alicia, and then you cook breakfast for them. What's with that?"

Mindy and Alicia exchanged a quick glance. Alicia's eye looked terrible. I was thinking it would be the biggest, darkest black eye imaginable. Purple, practically. I had one like it once.

I didn't look closely at Mindy. I didn't want to see straw in her hair.

"You know those guys?" I said.

"You could've stayed last night!" Mindy said. "They would've left."

"You could've left with me. I told you I didn't like the people at this party."

"And leave Alicia alone—like you left me. No, thanks."

"I didn't invite half the people that showed up," Alicia said mournfully, "and right now I've got a bigger problem.

What am I going to do about the garage? My folks will be back this afternoon."

I looked around and wondered what she was going to do about the kitchen, too.

"God," she moaned. "Those guys were supposed to help."

I let out a long sigh and shook my head. I hadn't even had a chance to tell Mindy about my house being spray painted and ask her what she knew about that. I still hadn't really looked at her to see if there was straw in her hair. I was thinking maybe I should ask her right now, *Did you sleep with one of those guys?*

But I tossed the idea. I needed to be alone with her for that.

I waved a hand in the air. "Hell! All right, look. You guys clean up this mess in the kitchen, and I'll start lugging stuff from the garage into the house. Just tell me where to put it."

• • •

"That was nice of you, Stony," Mindy said, sitting in my truck. "I'm sure Alicia appreciated your help."

It was three hours later.

I'd just settled behind the wheel of my truck after throwing five 50-gallon garbage bags of beer cans into the bed. "The garage looks a lot better. Smells better. I told Alicia to run the lawn mower in there a while. Make it smell like a garage again."

I started my truck and pulled out of the yard, Buddy barking at us.

"I appreciate the ride home," Mindy said.

I didn't hesitate. "What happened last night?"

I turned toward her, finally searching for straw in her hair, but all I saw were tears pooling in her eyes.

"It's not what you think."

"Tell me, anyway."

"I crashed on Alicia's bed in her room in the house. I don't know what time. Alone. I locked the door." Mindy wiped her eyes with the heel of her hand. "When I woke this morning, this guy was on the bed with me." She sounded as if she were reciting. "Nothing happened."

"Who is he?"

"Eric. The taller black-haired one. Eric Small."

"How'd he get into the room?"

"How do you suppose? He broke in. I lock my door at home, too. That doesn't stop my mom's boyfriends from trying to break in."

I shook my head, doubting Mindy was telling the truth.

"You shouldn't have gone home," she said.

"And you're telling me nothing happened."

"I passed out with my clothes on. He passed out, too. Clothes on."

I turned off the gravel road onto a blacktop heading toward town, fields of eight-foot-tall corn drying on either side of us.

I looked at her again.

She'd laced her hands in her lap, staring at them. Her jeans, T-shirt, and jacket looked pretty crummy, all rumpled and smudged with dirt. I still didn't see any straw in her hair.

I remained silent, both hands clamped tight on the top of the steering wheel.

Both passed out. What bullshit.

"You're mad, aren't you?" she said.

I didn't answer. I didn't know what I was feeling. Even if her story was true, if I was in love with her, I should have been butt-kicking furious—my girl in bed with another guy. But I wasn't furious. Really, I wasn't even jealous.

I was sad, that's it. Sad because I knew for sure I was losing someone who was once a big part of my life. But losing Mindy—wasn't that what I wanted? Why wasn't I smiling? Why was parting so painful?

"You could've been raped, you know that?"

"Whose fault, Stony?" Now I felt her eyes digging into me. "What did *you* do last night?"

I passed a road sign that said THOMPSONVILLE 2, only three cars on the road, both coming at me.

"I drove around a while. Went home. Went to bed."

"Why didn't you come back?"

"And find you in bed passed out with a guy? That's what I want to see."

We were silent for a few miles. Finally, Mindy wrung her hands and said, "You want to hear about Alicia's black eye?"

"Not interested."

I stopped for the first light in town. We weren't far from Mindy's house. "You ever leave the party last night?"

"What do you mean?"

"Leave. Go somewhere else. Like in a car."

"No. Why?"

"You were at Alicia's all the time?"

"*Duh,* Stony. That's where the party was."

I finally told her about my house being spray painted.

She sat back, staring at me, her jaw squared. "You think *I* did it? That's why you came after me this morning? That's what you wanted to know, not if I was okay?"

"I thought maybe it was your way of getting even with me for leaving you two nights in a row."

"You asshole! I did *not* spray paint your house."

I glanced at her. Tears ran down her cheeks again.

Once more, as I parked in front of her place, silence descended upon us.

Mindy lived with her mother, Ruby, in a matchbox house on a narrow, dead-end street in east Thompsonville. A beater of a Toyota sat in the gravel drive. No garage. Two

Harleys—one of them Ruby's—were parked in the tall grass in front of the house. Sometimes as many as four or five Harleys leaned in the yard.

After I parked, Mindy looked at me as if she was waiting for me to say something, tears still glittering in her eyes.

I knew what my lines should be. *I believe your story, babe. Can I see you tonight? I still love you . . . You're right. I shouldn't have left you alone last night. None of this would've happened. It's been all my fault.*

Mindy said, "Where are all the good times we had, Stony? Remember skinny-dipping in Miller's Pond? The deserted cabin we found at Wildcat Den?"

"Mindy . . ."

"Remember the janitors' broom closet at school? Where are those times, Stony?"

I shrugged.

"You going to call me?" She looked at me with her glassy eyes.

"Maybe it's like I told you last night, remember?"

"I've been trying to ignore that." Her eyes narrowed, and her nostrils flared. "It's that fucking Robyn Knight!"

"It's not!"

"What we had was good enough for you before her!" Gulping back more tears, Mindy opened her door, jumped out of the truck, and slammed the door. "I hate you!" penetrated the closed door and window.

I watched her bolt up the walk to her front door. I slumped at the wheel.

I shook my head.

I seriously doubted that Mindy was telling me the truth about sleeping with Eric. But I didn't know what to think about her denying spray painting my house.

I pulled away from the curb, hoping the spray painting had been a one-time thing only. Someone's not-so-funny idea of a joke.

Goodbye, Mindy.

thirteen

Monday morning, I was the last person in class to turn in Ms. Oberhaus's American Lit test. The other students had finished ten minutes ago and had started reading the introduction to the next unit: "New England Renaissance 1840–1855."

Before today, I was always the first person to hand in a paper. Practically blank. Then I'd go back to my seat and plunk my head down on my arm on the desk.

Surprised and pleased, Ms. Oberhaus looked up from her desk as I stapled my papers together and handed them to her.

"Well, Wendell," she said in her German accent, "I see four sheets of paper you have filled." She flipped the pages over. "Both sides. Tell me, Wendell, what does this mean?"

I smiled my first real smile since—I couldn't remember. "I studied. I didn't leave even one question blank." My chest puffed up a little.

"See what you are capable of if you work, Wendell?"

"Yes, ma'am."

"Most of us use less than fifty percent of our brain. Did you know that?"

"Yes, ma'am. Umm . . . my journal entries from the first unit?"

"What about them?"

"May I turn them in late? Get half credit or something? A few more points might help me pass."

"Perhaps, Wendell." She dropped my test into the wire basket on her desk with the others. "Let's see if what you have written is not all nonsense first."

• • •

I went all morning at school without seeing Mindy.

I really didn't expect her to show up at my locker before first period like she usually did to kiss me good morning, and I didn't expect her to show after third period, either, after her cigarette.

Actually, I was glad she was a no-show. Relieved, even.

But I did expect to see her darting by somewhere in the halls. When she didn't turn up by noon, I concluded she skipped school. She often missed Mondays.

. . .

Seventh period, Robyn arrived in the library just as I plunked down at the table in our special corner of the room. It was cool to think of it as "our" corner.

She was wearing black, including a thin, long-sleeved black sweater.

"Hi," I said, and delivered a smile that I hoped appeared genuine. It was meant to be.

Easing her books on the table, she sat down without a word, very efficient and cool.

"I passed my test this morning." My smile spread quickly across my face. "I know I did. Maybe an A. Depends what she gives me on the essays. She might let me make up my late journal entries."

"That's very good."

I whipped a sealed white envelope out of my back pocket. Tossed it in front of her on the table.

I said, "I figured you gave me three hours of instruction Saturday afternoon. Forty-five dollars' worth. It's all there. Count it."

She stared at the envelope a second, then shook her head.

"I don't want it."

"If it's not enough, I'll gladly pay more."

"That's not why I'm tutoring, to make money."

"I thought we had a deal. The money's why you agreed to meet me in the first place."

She shoved the envelope to me across the table. "I've changed my mind."

"Buy something nice for yourself. Or Logan."

When I worked in the bait shop for Mom, I never accepted wages. I always told Mom to take the money and buy something nice for herself, but I don't think she ever did. Still, I hoped Robyn would loosen up and say okay.

But Robyn, ignoring my request, leaned back in her chair and said, "Tell me about your test."

This girl was definitely stubborn. With my forefinger, I edged the envelope to the center of the table. Left it there.

"It wasn't all that hard," I said. "Lit terms. Biographical questions about the authors. A couple of essay questions."

"Tests aren't hard when you study." She placed her hand over mine, surprising me, totally, and my heart jumped. Her fingers were long and thin and cool. I surveyed her rings of turquoise and silver. "I'm glad you did well," she said softly. "I knew you would."

"Not without your help."

"You don't need me any longer. Read your assignments. Take notes. Write the journal entries. Study for your tests. You can do all that by yourself."

She gave my hand a quick squeeze, then pulled hers back.

I blinked. "What are you telling me?"

"You don't need me."

At that moment, I was thinking I wanted to flip her hand over and slide her sleeve up her arm to see if she was hiding needle marks. Or scars from needles. Or tattoos.

"You can't give up on me," I said. "How are you going to make a difference?"

"I'm not giving up on you. I should be helping someone who really needs help."

I nodded slowly. Leaned back in my chair. "You're afraid of me. Right? Afraid I'll get too close?"

Robyn lowered her head. Her long dark hair fell from its place behind her ears. "You're not going to make this easy for me, are you?"

"Or maybe it's me. I'm a Ridge Hick. I haven't done very well in school. You don't like football—the only thing I'm good at. I don't have any goals. No college plans."

Without looking up at me, Robyn said, "Your girlfriend Mindy wrote about you in her favorite stall again in the restroom."

I jerked back in my chair. "You're kidding."

"I'm not."

"Are you sure? Because she's not here today. At least, I haven't seen her."

"She must've been here early this morning."

I stared at the acoustic ceiling tiles with hundreds of little holes in them. This didn't make sense. Would Mindy come to school early Monday morning just to write about me on a restroom wall? I didn't think so. I looked at Robyn. "You go in there every day to see what she writes?"

"I go to the restroom every day." She stared at me.

My eyes dropped. "Sorry," I said. "I didn't mean to sound like this was your fault."

"She wrote about me, too."

I frowned. "She used your name?"

"'Tutor bitch' is what she called me. Said I'd stolen you away. You were too dumb to appreciate her. She made a list of the qualities you liked about her that you'll be missing."

I still couldn't believe this. "Like what?"

"Tight pussy, for one," Robyn said blankly, but her face was turning pink. "Big tits."

I winced and closed my eyes a second. "I'll talk to her!" I thumped my fist off the tabletop. "Don't be afraid of her. This won't happen ever again. I promise." Another fist-thump off the tabletop. "Believe me."

"What she wrote doesn't make any difference. We shouldn't see each other, anyway."

"Give me one good reason."

At that moment Mr. Pendergast, the school librarian, appeared at our table in the corner, glaring at us.

"What's all the racket?" he said. "I walk by and I hear someone yelling. Someone hitting a desk. Maybe slamming a book. Is that you, Wendell?"

He was a notorious jock-hater. A few years ago, a heavyweight wrestler named Todd Ram got so mad at him he tore the covers off all his long-overdue books. When Todd paid the fines, he had to pay for the books, too. Mr. Pendergast hadn't forgotten that hassle and apparently figured all jocks were stupid.

And I had been in trouble with Mr. Pendergast before, not for making a big disturbance in the library, though. Just for sleeping and snoring. Drooling a little on the tabletops.

I threw my palms up, begging for mercy, and flashed my best apologetic smile. "It won't happen again, sir. We'll be quiet."

Robyn stood, gathering her books. "It's all right, I was just leaving. I have a pass to my counselor's office."

Raising his head, Mr. Pendergast peered through the lower half of his glasses at the yellow hall pass she was holding. His eyes shifted to me. "You will not be allowed to work together in the library if you cannot remain quiet. Is that clear, you two?" Now he looked at Robyn.

"We won't be meeting after today," she said, and pressed her books to her chest, avoiding my eyes. She spun on her heels and left without saying goodbye.

"I trust you can behave yourself here alone till the end of the period," Mr. Pendergast said.

I didn't answer. I gritted my teeth. I was so pissed, so frustrated, I couldn't talk.

Why was Robyn Knight afraid of me? What was she hiding?

Something more than tattoos.

Go to hell, Mr. Pendergast!

The white envelope with Robyn's forty-five dollars in it remained on the table. I stuffed it into the back pocket of my jeans.

fourteen

After football practice that night, I ventured into McDonald's to have a few—final—in-your-face words with Mindy Hillman. She needed to know that if she ever wrote on a restroom wall about me, or someone I knew, I'd think seriously about wringing her neck.

But I didn't spot her behind the counter, in the kitchen, or at the drive-thru window.

"May I help you?" A counter girl I didn't recognize smiled at me.

The place was warm inside and smelled of French fries. My stomach was rumbling.

"Two double cheeseburgers, big fries, and a large Coke."

"For here or to go?"

"Here." I released my special get-acquainted smile for the new counter girl. "Mindy Hillman's not working? I'm a friend of hers."

"Uh-uh. She didn't show this afternoon. I got called in for her." The girl smiled back. Nice white teeth. "Will that be all, sir?"

"That's all." I thanked her, paid her, waited a minute or two for my food, then sat down and ate.

Something was wrong here. Mindy might skip school a lot, and she hated her job, but she never took off work. She needed the money. Her mom gave her nothing.

Something was definitely wrong.

• • •

On the way home, I stopped by Brian's house, a new brick home surrounded by oak trees on a hill, just on the edge of Hickory Ridge. The name of the street was Grandview Lane. Nice.

His mom let me in, said she was glad to see me, and ushered me to his bedroom. I plunked down in the chair in front of his computer desk. Posters of his old-time heroes hung everywhere on the walls: John Elway, Bart Starr, Terry Bradshaw, and lots more.

Trophies for baseball and football sat on every shelf and every other available flat space, like on his dresser and on top of the TV.

Dressed in jeans and T-shirt, he lay on his bed watching ESPN, remote in hand.

I said, "How you doin', dumbshit?"

For a moment, he didn't look at me. Then he said, "You ratted on me, didn't you?"

"They had it figured out, man. They're not stupid."

"I never figured you'd do that."

He sat up and jammed his pillow behind his back.

"You had to tell them your arm hurt," I said. "The sooner the better."

"Maybe at the end of the season."

"What? When you had stats? Or when your arm turned into a dishrag?"

He didn't look at me and started flipping through channels.

I said, "What happened exactly?"

He dropped the remote beside himself on the bed. "After practice the other night when I got home, I felt weak. Light-headed, I guess. I'd passed some blood. I didn't tell anyone."

"That was smart."

"I went to bed early. Got up during the night, and my mom heard me stumbling around in the bathroom. I finally told her I didn't feel very well."

"Jesus! I can't believe you waited so long."

"She took my temp—I didn't have a fever. But she couldn't find my pulse. Then I passed out. My folks called nine-one-one. They hauled me over to Genesis."

"Man, that was close. What's with the arm?"

As if to show me his elbow was okay, nothing to worry about, he laced his hands behind his head, his arms sticking out like chicken wings. "They think it's an inflammation of the elbow. I see an orthopedic specialist at the end of the week."

"You feel okay?"

"I've got no energy. Can't eat much of anything."

"You probably almost bled to death."

More channel flipping. Then, "You guys got the hell beat out of you Friday night."

"Tell me about it," I said and stared at the four-blade ceiling fan above his bed. "We fell apart. I missed a tackle that started them on a roll."

"You taking care of your English grade? I couldn't find my notes from last year."

I smiled and said, "Not to worry."

I explained what a great help Robyn had been, I thought she was a little different, but okay, and I might have aced a unit test. "But she doesn't want to tutor me anymore."

"You tried to get in her pants already?"

"I tried to be nice to her. Took her and her kid to Wildcat Den. She helped me study. Offered to pay her."

"Mindy wouldn't approve."

I didn't know what to tell him about Mindy. I didn't know what was up with her myself. So I let it go, and before I left, I said. "Hurry back, man. Even if you have to sit on the bench, you can help Lunardi. He needs it."

• • •

It was six-thirty when I walked into our empty house. Dad was at Foggy's—I saw his truck. And Mom was still working at the bait shop. First thing, I called Mindy's house, but no one answered. Next, I called Alicia, and a woman answered, probably her mother.

"I'm sorry," the woman said, "Alicia is grounded. She can't use the phone for the next month. Maybe for the rest of her life." The woman hung up with a *clunk!* before I could say who I was and that all I wanted was to ask if Alicia knew where Mindy was.

I hung up.

I gathered from the fact that Alicia was grounded that her parents must have found out about the party. Her black eye was a giveaway. And maybe I didn't find all the beer cans in the garage or around the yard, like in the bushes, flowers, and ditch by the road. I tried.

The phone rang.

I reached for it on the wall. This time I hoped it was Mindy. I stretched the coiled cord to the table. "Hello . . ."

"Wendell? This is Robyn."

Her voice, clear and firm on the phone, made my heart thump.

"Oh . . . hi." I tried to sound casual but couldn't hide my pleasure. "What's up?"

"I hated leaving you so abruptly this afternoon in the library, letting you take all the blame. I'm sorry. That wasn't right."

"Don't worry about it. I'm the one who made the noise, anyway. Let's find another place to work. The counselors' office maybe."

"Stony . . ." She hesitated, and now my heart did a complete flip-flop. That was the first time she'd called me *Stony.*

". . . I need to tell you something, and you must try to understand." I heard her take a breath. "I didn't want to tutor you."

"Why doesn't that surprise me?"

"Not a football player," she said. "I wanted to help someone who was desperate and needed me, not someone who I suspected was merely lazy."

"A 'lazy fuck,'" I reminded her, "is what you called me."

"Sorry about that." She cleared her throat. "I wanted to help a Vietnamese student, for example—a person with a language barrier."

"Then why did you help me?"

"Your coach said he needed you on the football team. Your counselor said if you got your grades up, you might be college scholarship material."

"What do you think?"

She brushed that aside. "Ms. Oberhaus said you had lots of potential. Nobody had reached it."

"Really?"

"She said you write okay, except for excessive use of sentence fragments, which shows your lack of discipline, but you could probably handle college work."

"She said that?"

"Yes. And that you'd be a challenge."

"Nobody lied, did they?"

"No."

"The thing is," Robyn said, "I wasn't—I'm not prepared for a personal relationship. I don't want one, and it has nothing to do with you."

"That's what you called to tell me?"

"Yes."

"Are you finished? That's it?"

"Yes. Except that I'm sorry. I . . . I think you're a nice person—not arrogant and overbearing like a lot of—"

She halted. Silence drifted in.

I said, "Like a lot of what—jocks?"

"I'm sorry," she said again. "I didn't mean to sound cruel."

"Well, good," I said. "Now that you've got that off your chest, how about if I take Logan and you fishing next Saturday afternoon?"

"Didn't you hear what I just said?"

"Who said anything about a relationship? I want to take you and Logan fishing. Has he ever been fishing? Have you?"

"Neither of us has."

"Are you going to deprive that boy of one of life's greatest pleasures? Not to mention yourself. Girls fish, you know. My mom does."

"Stony, there are lots of things you don't know about me."

"Same goes for me. Did you know I once caught a ten-pound walleye in the river? I was with my dad and grandpa. We got our picture in the paper. I've got the fish mounted. I'll show both to you sometime."

"Stony, I'm serious."

"I drive an old Ford pickup that has had only two owners. My grandpa and me. Want to hear something bad?"

"Stony, stop."

"I've been driving it since I was fourteen. Drove two years without a license. Only a learner's permit. Never got caught. What do you think of that?"

"If the circumstances were different, I might be interested in you, but not now, and that's all I can say."

"You don't have to tell me any secrets."

"And I'm not going to."

"I want to take you two guys fishing. That's all. I'm not expecting anything from you. What do you say? I'll pick you up at noon Saturday."

"I am *not* dating you."

"Fishing is not dating."

"What is it?"

"It's just *fishing!* Homecoming is dating. Dinner and a movie is dating."

"This isn't why I called," she mumbled.

"Dress Logan warm. A hooded sweatshirt, if you've got one. Just in case it's cloudy and windy on the river."

"Stony, I can't."

"I'll pick you up at noon. All right?" I held my breath a second, then aimed for her weak spot. "It's for Logan," I said. "Every kid should go fishing. He'll love it."

"Stony . . ."

"I'll guarantee we catch fish and that Logan has a good time. Think of that, if nothing else, a good time for Logan." That was almost unfair.

A major silence.

"What do you say, Robyn?"

"All right," she said. "Just this once. If it's sunny and warm."

Yes!

fifteen

Thursday. Brian was recovering and back in school, but Mindy wasn't.

I figured she must have quit, and I decided to check her locker at noontime.

The school lock was still on the door, but I knew the combination. I dialed the numbers, and when I swung the door open, I realized I'd been right. She'd cut and run. Only her books sat in her locker, top shelf. Her combs, brushes, fingernail polish, hair spray, and mirror had disappeared. Pictures of me on the door had been stripped away. She must have come to school Monday morning, ripped all that stuff down, then wrote on the restroom wall before ducking out.

And she must have quit without telling school officials. If they knew, her counselor would have picked up her lock and books.

I shrugged and closed the locker door.

I blew out a long breath.

What the hell!

Why did she do that? Not because of me, I hoped.

• • •

First thing after school, on my way to practice, I snagged Alicia by her locker. She wore a white patch taped over her black eye, and her cheek was swollen. I'll bet the side of her face felt like a melon.

"Did you know Mindy quit school?" I asked.

She looked at me with a one-eyed sneer. "For a jock, you're bright, Stony."

"Why quit? That's stupid." Alicia tried to turn away, but I grabbed her arm.

She seemed to take great delight in not speaking right away, making me wait, watching me squirm. "She's hooked up with Eric." Alicia tried to jerk free. "Let go of me! I'll scream, I really will!"

I released her.

"That creep she met at your party?"

Alicia nodded. "Eric Small. He's my cousin. He came up from Missouri for a while. She went back with him."

"She ran away with him?"

"Is that so hard to believe?"

"She quit school to run away with someone she doesn't know—damn right that's hard to believe."

"You didn't give her any other choice."

"Don't lay this on me."

"Why not? Figure it out, bright boy. She only stayed in school because of you. She hated living at home, her mom's boyfriends hitting on her all the time. What did you leave her?"

"She doesn't *know* the guy."

"She knows him from junior high—he went to school here a semester. He's older."

I thought about that.

"Ahh," I said, nodding. "Maybe that makes more sense. But not much."

"She wanted to marry you, Stony. She talked about it all the time. You and her living on the river. Raising a bunch of kids."

"We never made any plans like that."

"The other night she found out you're not the only stud around. She had a *big* time at my party."

I closed my eyes a moment.

There it was. The truth about Mindy and Eric at Alicia's party.

Alicia said, "You got muscles, you play football—I don't care. I always told her you were a lightweight."

I whirled and stalked off.

It was one thing to have Mindy out of my life, if she was, but I still cared enough for her to hope that her quitting school and hooking up with Eric weren't stupid choices she'd regret the rest of her life. All because of me.

Most of all, I hoped she was somewhere safe.

• • •

When I got home that night after football practice, Mom had already closed the bait shop. She was home and in a cleaning frenzy. It happened every two or three weeks when she finally couldn't stand the messy house any longer. If I knew the frenzy was coming, I tried to stay away. But once in a while, like tonight, when I was thinking of other things, I walked right into the middle of it, and I was trapped into helping.

I set my American Lit, history, and geography books on the kitchen table.

"Mom, I've had a long day. I have to study."

I wasn't ready to tell her about Mindy.

"You think my day hasn't been long?" Mom said. "You think I enjoy cleaning up after you and your dad after working all day?"

"Mom . . ."

"I want you to pick up all the clothes thrown around the house. Take them to the basement. Your dad's in one pile. Yours in another. I'll wash your dad's. You wash your own. Tonight. Then put them in the dryer. Then in your dresser. Tonight."

"Mom . . ."

"Tonight, Wendell!"

No use arguing with her. I'd never won an argument with my mom.

"Did you see your dad's truck?"

"I didn't look. Honest."

"Did you eat?"

"Um . . . I'm okay. I'm not hungry."

Then Mom said, "This fall when I close the bait shop for the winter, I might close it for good."

"What?"

"You heard me. For good. I can't handle it any longer. Then I'm dragging your dad out of Foggy's for good."

"He won't like that."

"And then we're all going to be home every night. The three of us. A family."

I was thinking that would be nice, but I didn't say it because I doubted it would come true.

"Like before what happened to Shane," Mom said, "when your dad didn't spend all his time in the tavern."

I said, "Have you told Dad you're going to close the bait shop?"

"Just made up my mind."

"Grandpa Stoneking started it himself with worms he caught in the grass at night with a flashlight and coffee can. He seined Indian Creek for minnows and crawdads."

"I know. But it takes all my time. Leaves me no time for the things I need to be doing. Want to be doing."

I heaved out a sigh.

My family was far from perfect, I realized, but we all cared for each other. We were still together. I was grateful for that. That was more than Mindy had going for her.

"I'll sweep and vacuum, too," I told Mom.

• • •

In American Lit the next morning, when Ms. Oberhaus handed back my test paper, I wouldn't have been able to stop my smile if I tried.

"An A-minus, Wendell," Ms. Oberhaus said. "Quite remarkable. And to think all this time you could have been earning As. Last year, even—and you wouldn't be taking this course over."

"Does it mean I'm going to pass mid-quarter?"

"Not yet. One passing grade does not turn a sow's ear into a silk purse."

Ms. Oberhaus's gray eyes twinkled a little. I didn't know she had a sense of humor, and I said, "Analogy? Right?"

"Very good, Wendell."

I cleared my throat and prepared to display my best grammar. "*May* I write my missed journal entries and turn them in late for partial credit?"

Ms. Oberhaus nodded. "Yes, Wendell. That would be appropriate, I think."

• • •

Seventh period I rushed to the library, hoping to find Robyn and show her my test. I was thinking she might be tutoring a new student. Or maybe she'd come in to use the library for her own studying, figuring she'd no longer have to put up with me.

As I pushed through the gate that triggered an alarm if you're stealing a book, I spotted her at a long table by the windows, reading the daily newspaper, the sun streaming in, gleaming off her long black hair.

Before she had a chance to look up, I slipped into a chair and sat down opposite her, my test paper rolled in my hand. I figured we still had a minute or two to talk before Pendergast announced, "Quiet now, people."

"Hey," I said. "Ask me what I got on my lit test."

She grinned, tucking her hair behind her ears. "A-plus. What are you doing here?"

"A-minus! Still think I'm some lazy fuck jock?"

"The thought never crossed my mind."

"Irony? Right?"

"Maybe."

I smoothed out my paper in front of her on the table. She studied it, nodding her head approvingly when she read my essay answers.

"Very impressive." She handed the paper back. "I told you she'd ask about allegory, and this paper proves you don't need a tutor."

"Give me your phone number."

"Why?"

"So I can call you Saturday afternoon. What if it's raining on the river? How can I call to make different plans?"

"No need to. Just don't show up."

"What if it's sunny on the river but raining in town? I'll show up and you won't be ready. Logan will be pissed . . . Sorry about that." I realized my voice was getting a little loud. I glanced over my shoulder for Pendergast. He wasn't in sight.

"I haven't told Logan I'm thinking about going," she said.

"Why not?"

"So he won't be disappointed in case we don't."

I made a fist and rapped my knuckles off the table. "How about your phone number? Just in case."

"I told you, if the weather's bad, don't show. Shhh. We better be quiet now."

"Don't *be* that way!" I said, my voice louder than before.

And suddenly Mr. Pendergast stood at the end of the table, his arms crossed. "Mr. Stoneking," he said, "I believe you have finally made it necessary for me to banish you to the study hall for the rest of the semester."

"You're kidding. What am I doing wrong? We can talk now. The period hasn't started. Everyone else is talking."

"No one else is talking. The period started some time ago."

I glanced at the big, round wall clock above the entrance door. The period had started exactly a minute ago.

"I'm sorry," I said.

"I warned you yesterday about raising your voice in the library. Are you harassing this young lady?"

I looked at Robyn. "Am I harassing you?"

"He's not," she told Mr. Pendergast.

"To the study hall, anyway, Mr. Stoneking. And I don't want to see you back here before second semester."

"I'm kicked out?"

"Precisely."

Robyn said, "That's not fair." The color in her cheeks rose. "Are you picking on him because he's an athlete?"

My ears perked. Man, she was sticking up for me!

But Mr. Pendergast ignored her.

"Make sure, Mr. Stoneking," he said, "you arrive at the study hall each seventh period. I'll be checking on you. Personally."

"He wasn't doing anything," Robyn said. "I was talking, too."

"It's all right," I said. I shoved my chair back, rose, and smiled my anger-hiding smile. "Whatever pleases you, Mr. Pendergast, sir. Have a good day. Sir." I looked at Robyn. "I'll see you Saturday. Rain or shine."

sixteen

Friday night's football game was on the road. Ninety miles away. Lynn Center. Record 2-2. A dangerous ball club, especially at home.

All week at practice Coach Maddox stressed the need for us Tigers to put the Pleasant View loss behind us. Our destiny as a team remained in our own hands. With a 3-1 record, we still had a shot at the conference title, especially if we won the rest of our games, including the final game of the season against Farmington, currently 4-0.

If we beat Farmington at the end of the regular season and if both schools owned an 8-1 mark, we would automatically qualify for the state tournament. We would be conference co-champions, but our having beaten the Farmington Flyers the final game of the season would give us the nod for tournament play.

Then the playoffs. Four wins would propel us to the state championship, laying the trophy in our hands. A lot of *ifs*. But it was all possible. Especially since Lunardi, with Brian's help, was showing a lot of promise in practice.

Not much talk among the guys on the bus as it ground its way to Lynn Center on a hilly, winding, two-lane strip of highway. The sun dipped slowly behind river bottom trees. Hundreds of acres of dried corn and soybeans stood in farmers' fields, ready for harvest. I figured the night would be crisp and clear. Maybe cold. Great for football.

I sat next to Brian and we chatted. Dressed in his street clothes, he was feeling low. He'd had a MRI and a bone scan of his arm. Both showed nothing but a severe inflammation in his elbow. No evidence of a stress fracture. An operation wouldn't be necessary. Nothing radical like that. The orthopedic doctor told him the best thing he could do now was rest the arm. But he was out for the rest of the season, his reign as quarterback for the Thompsonville Tigers over. What lousy luck.

Still, just sitting on the bench in his street clothes, hanging tough, he'd be an inspiration to the rest of us.

I said, "You got good stats from last year, this year, too. Take care of that arm, even if you don't get a scholarship, you can walk on somewhere."

"That's the same thing Maddox and my dad told me." He stretched his right arm out. "I'm going to do my best in rehab. I'll give up baseball."

The bus bumped and groaned along, as if the driver was aiming at every pothole in the road.

"You want to hear something Mindy did, something not very bright?"

"What? She drag you into the janitors' closet again?"

"She quit school. Ran off to Missouri with some guy she met at Alicia's party."

"You're kidding me! All of a sudden like that?"

"I can't believe it either."

"What the hell did you do?"

"We'd been fighting lately. Last weekend, I left her twice at parties. She got pissed. I'm sure she cheated on me. She split."

He looked at me. "You don't sound broken up."

I shrugged in my shoulder pads. "It's just that I wonder what's going to happen to her."

"You're better off without her."

"I think she wanted to get married. Have kids."

"Man, I'm not ready for that."

"Me either. I haven't got myself figured out. Let alone life with another person."

"Things get scary, don't they—school, girls, football?"

"Especially when you try to figure out a future for yourself."

"Keep your grades up," he said and grinned. "You're not really all that stupid."

"Like popping pills was brilliant, dumbshit." I'd already told him about my acing my American Lit test.

"Stay focused," he said, "and anything's possible. That's what my dad says."

I loved my dad, but he wasn't one to offer advice about life like that.

Brian and I talked a little more. I told him how Robyn had maybe changed her mind about me. I was taking Logan and her fishing tomorrow afternoon.

As the bus trudged along I wondered, *Is it possible? Can I make a change?* The challenge seemed frightening. I mean, I'd studied for only one test. College, a totally different environment, would mean studying all the time. In Hickory Ridge on the river, life was easy. Hunting and fishing whenever I wanted. A job in the quarry. No fear of failure. Keep smiling.

But what if change was possible? What if I could do it? *What if?*

· · ·

The game was ugly.

Catching us off guard, rain had soaked Lynn Center all day, stopping only an hour before game time. The night was cold, the field a pig sty. Players slipped, fell, and slid in the mud as if they had no sense of balance, as if they were starring in a comedy.

We fumbled the slippery ball away four times in the first half to end long, muddy drives. We finally settled for a twelve-yard field goal late in the second quarter, giving us a 3-0 lead.

But the Lynn Center Greyhounds answered four plays later when their tailback squirted fifty-three yards off tackle and skated across the goal line for a TD. Two guys decked me on my face in the mud on that play. The PAT sent us into the locker room trailing 7-3 at halftime.

Coach Maddox was furious. He stormed up and down among us mud-caked players sitting on wooden benches in the visitors' locker room, heads hanging low.

"Lynn Center's not going to hand us a victory. They don't feel sorry for us. We're down, and they're going to kick us in the balls. Just like Pleasant View did last week.

Thirty-five to zip. Remember that? That's the way life is. You guys have got to pick yourselves up and kick some ass. What's it going to be? It's your call!"

We responded with a workman-like, fifteen-play drive to start the second half. All on the ground, the drive ate up seven minutes and produced a touchdown and extra point for a 10-7 Tiger lead. The margin held up into the fourth quarter when we kicked another field goal, boosting our edge to 13-7.

Then with two minutes left in the contest, the Greyhounds drove to our five-yard line. First down. A touchdown and an extra point would give them a 14-13 victory, but on second-and-five, I crushed the Greyhound ball carrier with a driving tackle. The ball popped into the air, hit the mud with a smack, didn't bounce, and three of our guys pounced on it, ending the threat and protecting our 13-7 victory.

I'd never felt more thankful after a game.

"Great effort," Coach Maddox said to me as I trudged off the field with the team. "We needed a big play. You drilled that guy."

All the players congratulated me as we piled wet, muddy, and shivering onto the bus for the two-hour ride home.

"You done good," Brian said. "You're a hero."

But I didn't feel like a hero. My teeth chattering, I felt cold and lonely, and despite the victory, there was no celebrating on the bus. No bus-rocking singing of the school song. No boisterous window-rattling cries of "WE ARE NUMBER ONE!" We all sank silently into our seats, heads down, helmets in our laps, the smell of grass, mud, and rain clinging to our bodies.

We all knew we had a long way to go before we were even close to being state champs. And, of course, we'd have to do it without Brian's play.

I slept most of the way home, my head feeling like a balloon bobbing about on a stick. Whenever the bus hit a pothole or made a sharp turn, I woke with a start. When the team got back to school, no one mentioned getting together for a beer, and I didn't ask. We did the Romp in the Woods thing only after home games. Brian said he was beat. He was heading straight home. I showered quickly—hot, hot water—and changed into my street clothes.

It was one-thirty when I left the locker room.

No Mindy waiting for me in the parking lot tonight.

I remembered how her lips would feel on my forehead, my cheeks, my mouth. Everywhere. But I shook my head, scattering the thoughts.

Home and to bed. Game films at ten in the morning. Then an afternoon on the river with Robyn and Logan.

Suddenly I wondered if Lynn Center's rain was pushing northeast. Would it hit Thompsonville later today, dousing my plans?

In the parking lot before I climbed into my truck, I looked at the sky. Black. Cloudy. Not a star. No moon.

Not good.

• • •

When I parked my truck in front of my house and got out, the dim streetlight cast a yellow glow over the intersection and Vernon Purdy's coonhound howled up the street. But the sound was way too close, as if the dog was loose and on a scent. He did that once in a while—got loose and chased coons all around the neighborhood, knocking over garbage cans, treeing one, barking, waking people up, getting them mad as hell at old Vernon. One night, coming home late like this, I was able to coax the dog to me and put him back in his pen.

I walked to the corner, peered down the street, hoping to catch a glimpse of Bruno and whistle him down.

But what I glimpsed was not a dog. The sight forced me to jump back and suddenly made my skin crawl.

Freshly spray painted on the patch of siding I'd painted white the other day was a red heart dripping three drops of blood. Painted exactly as before.

I whirled.

A feeling that someone was watching gripped me. Maybe the painter just finished. Was he hiding behind our oak tree on the corner? Or hiding in that parked car down the street? Would he call out to me?

But all was quiet on the street except for Purdy's dog, the wailing farther away now.

I turned to stare at the heart. I swallowed. I knew Mom and Dad were in bed by this time, having wandered home from Foggy's without seeing this. Thank God. If Mom had seen it, she'd be up waiting for me now, going crazy, lights on in the house.

The fact that my house had been spray painted a second time meant the first time was no accident. My house hadn't been chosen randomly out of the neighborhood just for fun. Someone was definitely sending me a message.

Couldn't be Mindy. She'd left town.

Unless she really hadn't left yet, and this was her parting shot.

That's the only reasonable thing I could think of.

Quickly and quietly I hauled the paint and brush from the basement. In ten minutes, in the dark, I slapped enough paint across the graffiti to paint the entire side of the house.

I couldn't tell Mom and Dad about this second painting, but somehow I had to find the painter and break his arms. Or hers. Maybe I'd have to climb the tree on the corner and wait for the bastard. Not a very practical idea, but what else could I do? I was desperate.

Satisfied with my paint job, I returned the paint and brush to the basement and stole silently upstairs to my room. I stripped to my jockey shorts and fell facedown on my bed spread-eagled, but I couldn't sleep.

Someone was after me.

And I didn't know for sure who. Or why.

seventeen

Jumping out of bed at eight o'clock Saturday morning, I dressed in jeans and a T-shirt and raced outside to see if the red heart had bled through my paint job. Last night in the dark, I couldn't tell much.

With gray clouds hanging low in the sky, dripping rain, I stood on the sidewalk, arms folded across my chest, shoulders hunched against the drizzle, and looked hard at the side of the house, trying to view my paint job from all angles. No matter where I stood, or how I craned my neck, I could see no bleed through. Thank God.

When would the painter strike again?

Who was the asshole?

The brilliant white patch of paint on the side of the house looked pretty stupid. How long before the neighbors started asking Mom and Dad questions? Or making smart remarks. "I like the color. Run out of paint?"

As I drove to school through the drizzle for game films, the weatherman on the radio predicted sunny skies by noon and a sixty-five- to seventy-degree temperature by mid-afternoon.

Hear that, Robyn and Logan?

Perfect!

If the guy wasn't lying.

· · ·

At noon, after game films, when I parked in front of Robyn's sister's house, I smiled to myself. Clouds had drifted away, and the sun popped out, warm on my left shoulder and arm, hanging out my truck window. The air smelled fresh.

The moment I stopped my truck at the curb, Robyn raced out of her sister's house and across the walk to meet me.

"You and Logan ready?"

"I thought it would rain all day."

"You have to put more faith in the weatherman. And me."

"Where's the boat?"

"Left it at the boat landing on the river. No need to pull it into the city and back again."

"I wanted to see it. Is it big enough? Is it safe?"

"A seventeen-foot flat bottom. Five feet across. You can dance in it." No need to tell her the seventy-five horse Merc that powered the boat could shoot it down the river like a missile. "Got life jackets and cushions. Fire extinguisher and horn. Everything according to Coast Guard standards."

She nodded approvingly.

"See you won last night," she said.

"Barely." I figured now was as good a time as any to tell her about Mindy. "You won't have to worry about Mindy writing about you in the restroom anymore. She dropped out of school and ran away to Missouri with a guy."

"You're kidding?" Genuine concern registered in Robyn's voice. "Why?"

"She's got her reasons, I guess."

"What's she going to do?"

"I don't know."

"Something must've upset her."

"She found this other guy and took off." My arm out the window, I slapped the side of the truck. "Let's go!"

"All right," Robyn said. "I'll get Logan ready."

• • •

"That's where my dad works," I said, as I drove along Highway 22, past the gravel pits.

"My daddy's in jail," Logan announced. He was buckled into his car seat between Robyn and me, wearing jeans and a hooded sweatshirt. "He hurt Mommy."

Silence crept into the truck's cab.

I knew I'd heard Logan correctly, but I kept my eyes focused on the road. When I finally turned toward Robyn, she was staring at me from under her floppy felt hat.

She said, "I don't believe in lying to children. Telling them whatever they're able to understand when they ask is the better way, I think."

I would have liked to ask more about Logan's daddy, but I elected not to, not in front of the boy.

"Look, Mommy! Trucks!" Logan squealed.

He pointed out the window at the array of gravel trucks and bulldozers parked around the quarry offices and yard.

"Big trucks," Robyn said.

"Big!" Logan repeated.

"I worked here during the summer," I said. "I drove a forklift. Sometimes I work on weekends after football's over."

"Is that what you're going to do after you graduate?"

"I still don't know."

"You should explore all your options."

"You sound like my counselor." I cleared my throat. "May I ask you a question?"

"Go ahead."

Putting everything I'd like to know about her into a single question would be impossible, and I had a feeling she might not want to talk about herself in front of Logan, anyway, so I said, "Tell me about your mom and dad, and your sister."

Robyn didn't speak right away, but seemed to consider her answer carefully, as if being selective about what she wanted to tell me. Finally she said, "My dad's in management with a big insurance company in Connecticut. My mom's a history professor at a local college. My sister graduated from there and went to Peru with the Peace Corps. She met a guy from Thompsonville who was also in the Peace Corps."

"You're kidding. Thompsonville?"

"That's right. They got married and returned here."

"What's his name?"

Logan pointed again. "Look, Mommy!"

"I see that," Robyn said. "Big hole in the ground. Big, big hole."

"That's where gravel and cement come from," I said. "That hole is three hundred feet deep and a half mile square. Getting bigger all the time. What's your brother-in-law's name?"

"Tom Packer. My sister's name is Elaine. They both teach Spanish at Blackhawk Junior College." She tilted her head and gave me an are-you-satisfied look.

I was trying like crazy to think of someone I knew named Packer but came up blank.

She said, "Now you know everything about my family and me."

"Not quite," I said. "But that'll do for a while."

. . .

The Mississippi River was beautiful.

Clouds had scurried away, leaving the sky arched overhead pure and blue. The sun glimmered off the water, and up and down the river, trees wore gold, scarlet, and brown. A cool breeze blew.

I'd work in the quarry forever, I guessed, so I could stay on this river. Huck Finn and me.

I seated Robyn and Logan in the bow of the boat, a cooler full of pop in the center.

Secured snugly in their life jackets, my passengers regarded me with watchful eyes as I untied the bowline and stepped off the dock into the boat, rocking it. Both gripped the gunwales.

"You're not going to go too fast, are you?" Robyn said.

I eased into the seat at the console and pushed the tilt/trim lever, lowering the Merc into the water. I slipped the throttle into neutral, turned the key, and fired up the motor. It grumbled impatiently, eager to roar. I looked across the river. A half mile wide at this point, the river was so calm in the afternoon sunlight it looked like a lake. Perfect conditions to crank up the ol' Merc and really fly.

"How fast are you going to go?" Robyn said.

"Not too fast," I said. "Just fast enough."

"Fast!" Logan's blue eyes suddenly danced bravely. "I want to go fast."

As the boat drifted down river away from the dock, I motioned to Logan. "Come sit by me. I'll let you drive."

Robyn's protest was quick and firm. "Stony, no!"

"It's okay," I said. "I'm just going to let him put his hands on the steering wheel." I motioned to him again. "C'mon, Catfish, help me drive."

"My name's not Catfish."

"I know. Help me drive anyway. Let him go, Robyn. It's how my dad and grandpa taught me."

She released Logan. Arms out, hardly able to stand up bundled in his life jacket, he staggered three steps toward me. I caught him and wedged him between my legs on the seat where he could grip the steering wheel with me.

"Take your hat off, hang onto it," I told Robyn.

Inching the throttle forward, I turned the boat and pointed its bow across the river. Then I gave the throttle a nudge. The boat jumped to the surface, planing easily as Robyn's eyes grew wide and Logan beat his palms on the steering wheel. At half throttle, on a bright, calm day, the boat glided across the river like a skater over ice.

On the other side of the river, I slowed the boat to a crawl as I slipped it through a narrow slot in a bank of trees that opened up into a maze of backwater ponds, channels, and sloughs.

"I've been fishing these backwaters for years," I said. "Started with my dad when I was a kid."

"It's beautiful here," Robyn said, relaxed now and smiling, as Logan and I guided the boat along at a snail's pace. "Like another world. Stumps. Lily pads. Tree limbs hanging down to the water." She plunked her hat back onto her head.

"Bound to find some crappies," I said. "What do you think, Logan? You want to go fishing?"

Logan nodded and clapped his hands. "I want to go fishing! I want to catch them all."

As I banked the boat around a bend into a sparkling pond, a flock of ducks sounded off in alarm. *Quack! Quack! Quack!* Their wings beat frantically and their feet paddled hard as they took flight from the water.

"Look," Robyn cried. "Ducks! A hundred of them!"

"Ducks!" Logan echoed. "Look at the ducks! They're flying."

"Headed south for the winter," I said. "Stopped here to rest."

Robyn watched the ducks skim the treetops and disappear in the blue sky. "Ducks all gone," she said to Logan.

"Donald Duck?" Logan said.

"His cousins," Robyn said.

Studying the depth finder, I anchored over a fifteen-foot hole off a narrow point where I had always caught fish. In fact, the depth finder showed fish suspended at eight feet.

I'd already rigged poles for Logan and Robyn with spincast reels, red-and-white slip bobbers, and tiny gold hooks. I baited the hooks with minnows and cast out, one pole in each hand.

Logan watched every move I made.

I handed a pole to him, then one to Robyn.

"Keep your eye on that bobber, Catfish," I told Logan. "When it goes under, give a yank and reel in! Sit here in the center. Reel like this." I guided Logan's hand through a few cranks on the reel. Then I shifted to Robyn. "Same goes for you. Watch the bobber. Yank when it goes under. Not too hard. Crappies have a paper-thin mouth."

"Aren't you going to fish?" Robyn said.

"Not today."

I knew if the crappie were hitting, I'd have my hands full taking fish off, rebaiting, and untangling lines.

I glanced at Logan, then at Robyn. Each sat alert as a cat watching a mouse. The ride across the river and the breeze had painted roses on their cheeks.

Twenty feet from the boat, Logan's bobber dipped.

"Watch your bobber!" I told him.

It dipped again, disappearing, then popped to the surface.

I reached around Logan and grabbed his hands as the bobber skated five feet across the water then vanished.

Logan and I yanked together, and with a little help from me, Logan reeled in a ten-inch black crappie, bouncing it off the side of the boat before landing it, the fish dropping at his feet.

Logan jumped about, his face bright with excitement. "I caught a fish!" he cried. "A big one!"

"Beautiful, isn't he?" I said, twisting the hook out of the wiggling fish's lip, holding it up for Robyn and Logan to inspect. Logan backed away, hands at his mouth.

"What are we going to do with it?," Robyn said.

"Release it," I said. "Unless you want to take a mess of fillets home. I'll clean them for you."

Robyn shook her head.

"What do you think, Catfish? You want to hold him?"

Logan backed away again. "No," he said.

"We'll let him go," I said. "Say goodbye, fish."

"Goodbye, fish," Logan said, as I slipped the fish back into the water. "Where's your bobber?" I asked Robyn.

"What? Oh! I don't know."

In the excitement, she hadn't thought of her own bobber or the pole in her hand. Suddenly her bobber exploded to the surface, then plunged out of sight again, bending her pole, line snapping taut.

"I got one!" Robyn cried, and bolted up.

"Might be a bass!" I said. "Sit down! Keep your rod tip pointed up."

But she didn't sit.

Standing, heaving back on her pole with all her might, Robyn ripped the hook from the fish's mouth. The sudden release of pressure on the line sent her flailing backward. The bobber, sinker, and hook snapped back at her as if they'd been fired from a cannon, sailing over the top of her head. Catching her, I wrapped my arms around her waist, barely saving her from falling over the side into the water. Instead, we tumbled into the bottom of the boat at Logan's feet.

"You all right?" I asked, my face so close to hers I felt her warm breath on my lips. My heart was hammering. I wanted to kiss her. Our eyes locked for a second, and I knew she knew what I was thinking.

"Yes, I'm all right," she said quickly, pushing me away. "Except you're practically on top of me."

"Mommy's hat's gone!" Logan said in the background.

I realized this was the wrong place and time for a kiss. Nearly breathless, I scrambled to my knees and helped Robyn into the boat's center seat. Her face was flushed.

I expected her to be furious for my landing on her like that and thinking what I was thinking. I expected to get called for piling on, but she surprised me, saying, *"Damn!* I lost my fish, didn't I? What was it? *Shit!"*

As she glanced at Logan, her hand flew to her mouth. She was apparently hoping he hadn't heard his mom say a bad word.

"The way it took your line," I said, "maybe it was a bass. Two, three pounds."

"Your hat, Mommy!" Logan said again, and pointed at the water.

"Oh, my God!" Robyn said, grabbing at her head.

Brim down on the water's surface, Robyn's felt hat was floating slowly and silently away.

"You nearly got hit in the head with a bobber, sinker, and hook," I said, "and your hat flew off when we fell."

"Can we get my hat?" Robyn pleaded.

"No sweat."

I picked up Logan's pole, cast the line thirty feet out, over the top of the hat, and reeled in slowly. The bobber slipped over the hat, but the hook snagged it, and I handed the pole to Robyn.

"Reel in slowly," I said. "Might be your biggest catch of the day."

"Mommy caught her hat!" Logan said in amusement, and we all laughed.

eighteen

After the snag-a-hat adventure, I estimated Robyn and Logan caught over thirty crappie, most of them big, fat, ten- to twelve-inch fish, perfect for filleting and eating. But we released them.

By four in the afternoon, when a few clouds drifted across the blue sky, blotting out the sun, the air turned chilly, and I realized it was time to take my passengers back.

I knew they'd had a great time on their first fishing experience in the Mississippi River. They'd been laughing and joking all afternoon, each claiming to have caught the most fish. And the biggest.

As I pulled the anchors, I declared the competition a tie.

I wanted desperately to take Robyn out tonight. A movie, maybe. Logan could come, too. We'd see a film for kids. Have pizza after.

I motored us slowly back across the river, a chop on the water now, a chilly breeze in our faces. Logan helped me steer. After we docked, and I trailered the boat, I secured the fishing poles and anchors and plugged in the trailer lights. Holding Logan in her arms, Robyn followed me around so the boy could watch everything I was doing to make the boat ready for towing.

"We're ready to go," I announced, and leaned against my truck. "We'll drop the boat at my house. Then take you back to the city."

"Fine," Robyn said.

Logan rubbed his eyes and yawned loudly. "I want to fish again."

"You bet," I said. "Maybe next time I'll take you for a long, long ride on the river."

"We've had an awesome time." Robyn shifted Logan in her arms to her other hip. "Haven't we, Logan?"

The boy nodded his head, and I gave him a tweak on his cheek.

Then Robyn said, "Would you like to come over tonight, Stony? I'll make pizza."

I blinked. "You mean . . . to your sister's house?"

"You have something else planned?"

"No, I don't." I smiled broadly. "Honest. I was thinking almost the same thing. You and me . . . pizza . . ."

She gave me a look. "Don't let your imagination run wild."

"I won't."

"Pizza is my way of saying thanks. Nothing more."

"That's understood."

Logan started sucking his thumb.

"He only does that when he's really tired," Robyn said.

"I sucked my thumb till I was nearly six, I think."

"I'm tired, Mommy."

"I know you are, honey." Then to me, "Call me after you get home. I have to check with Elaine and Tom first. They're going out for the evening, but I don't think they'll mind if you come over."

"The number's in the book? Tom Packer?"

"It's unlisted." She repeated the number twice so I could commit it to memory. Finally.

• • •

That night I stuffed myself with Robyn's delicious deep-dish sausage, cheese, and mushroom pizza. Later, I sprawled on the soft carpet in the TV room with Logan, a pillow for each of us, watching a film I've never seen before, *The Lion King*. I remembered Shane was crazy about *Charlotte's Web* and would watch it five times a day every day if Mom let him.

Logan must have seen this one a million times. He knew every plot twist, quoted dialogue, and didn't hesitate to keep me informed about what was going to happen next.

Robyn curled in a lounge chair, her legs and feet tucked beneath her, watching with us. I wondered how many times she'd seen the film with her son.

Tom and Elaine had a nice house full of new furniture with plush carpeting and expensive-looking wall pictures with lights above them. I was embarrassed earlier when I dropped the boat at my house and Robyn saw the shack I live in. She didn't ask about the bright three-foot-square patch of white painted on the side of the house, and I didn't volunteer an explanation. Your house being spray painted isn't something you talk about much.

When the film was finished, Robyn clapped her hands, popped out of the chair, and said, "All right, Logan! It's nine o'clock, sweetheart. Straight to bed. You've already had your bath."

"I want to watch it again."

"Not tonight."

"I want to, Mommy."

"I said no."

I said, "Fishermen need their sleep. You better go to bed. Give me five, first."

"Logan, tell Stony thank you for a nice time today," Robyn said.

"Thank you," Logan said shyly and smacked my open palm with his own.

"You're welcome, Catfish." On my knees, I kissed him on the forehead. "'Night."

"Can we fish again?"

"Any time."

"Are you going to be my daddy now?" Logan said.

"Logan!" Robyn cried, her eyes jumping from the boy to me.

I sat back on my haunches. "I don't think so."

"I want a daddy."

"Logan! Stop that!" Robyn led him firmly by the hand down the hallway to the bathroom.

When she came back in ten minutes, I was sitting on the couch, remote control in hand, skipping through the channels. I stopped at the History Channel.

"Are you one of those?" Robyn said. "A channel surfer?"

"I'm afraid so," I said. "Anything special you want to watch?"

She shook her head. "Logan really likes you."

"I like him, too."

I hoped she would sit next to me on the couch, but she settled on the floor, next to my legs, and stretched hers out in front of her.

"I never went to bed so easy," I said. "My brother, either."

The narrator on TV was talking about some plane lost in the desert in Africa during World War II, the *Lady Be Good.*

"Logan's pretty good about it," Robyn said. "I let him watch too much TV, though. I should read to him more."

"If your sister and her husband work, who watches him during the day?"

"Daycare. My father pays for it. I try to spend all my time with Logan when I'm not in school. It's so good he got to do something different today. In a boat. Fishing. He loved it." She turned to look up at me. "You still have a million questions about me, don't you?"

"I don't even know where to begin." I bent and kissed her on the forehead.

"You shouldn't do that," she said.

"What?" I smiled and kissed her again on the same spot. "That?"

She smiled back. "Your smile is contagious." She looked away from me and brought her legs up, hugging her knees. "A girl who has a child before she leaves high school faces a harsh future. Did you know that?"

"I guess, but I haven't thought about it much."

"Less education. Fewer chances of getting a good job. Dismal prospects for a happy marriage. I don't want any of that to happen to me. I'm fighting as hard as I can to make sure none of it does."

I wondered what she was trying to tell me. *There's no place for you in my life, Stony.*

"I was fourteen when Logan was born," she said. "Thirteen when I got pregnant. I have a rich family, but I felt bored. Neglected, even. I started looking for thrills and started making some very dumbass choices. Want to see?"

"What?"

"Something stupid."

Her back toward me, she leaned forward and hiked up her shirt, exposing a huge tattoo on her back, a green dragon with gleaming black eyes and ivory-like fangs and claws, a dragon blowing fire from its mouth, smoke from its nostrils.

She wasn't wearing a bra. The green, red, black, and ivory colors were vivid against the background of her pale flesh. I felt like if she inhaled and exhaled, the dragon would come alive.

My dumb mouth hung open, and I blinked and blinked until I thought my eyes would water. Mindy hadn't lied to me after all.

Yanking her shirt down, Robyn said, "You can't believe I'd do that, can you?"

"I—I didn't expect it."

"Is it beautiful or ugly?"

"I can't tell. Really."

"I thought it was beautiful once."

Maybe she'd done a lot of other reckless things. And now I understood why she was so protective of Logan, wondering if my boat was safe, if there would be snakes and ticks in the woods. She didn't want her boy to flirt with danger like she probably had.

I scratched my bristly head.

"Leaves you a little speechless," she said, "doesn't it?"

"Has Logan ever seen that?" I said, afraid to ask why she'd got the tattoo.

"No. But someday I'll have to show him. I can't hide it forever."

I poked the remote's power button and the TV went black, leaving the room bathed in the glow of a single light from an end table. I eased off the sofa and sat next to her on the floor.

I wondered about needle marks on her arms. She'd worn long-sleeve shirts all day. And did she have other tattoos in more private areas of her body?

"Alan didn't want me to have the baby," Robyn said. "But I'd never kill a human being."

"Alan?"

"Alan Blythwood. Logan's dad. When I told him I was going to have the baby, he freaked. He was sixteen." Robyn brushed her hair back, tucking it behind her ears. "He's terribly jealous and possessive and wanted to share me with no one. Not even his own son. I broke up with him. My parents thought I should have Logan adopted out, but I couldn't do that, either."

She felt warm next to me, but none of our body parts were touching.

"One night when Logan was six months old, I was home with him and Alan broke into the house. He ripped the phone out of the wall. He had a gun. He was high. Marijuana laced with cocaine. He wanted me to leave Logan and my parents and run away with him."

"How old was this guy, did you say?"

"Seventeen then," Robyn said. "I told him I'd never go with him. He was crazy that night."

"Sounds like it."

"He made me undress in front of him. He fired the gun in the air to show he meant business. He forced me onto the bed. Raped me. He left bruises on my throat."

I made a painful face and shook my head.

"If I didn't go with him, he said he'd kill Logan."

"Jesus Christ!"

"But he let me live, so I could be miserable the rest of my life—like he'd be without me. I don't know how long he was there. Neighbors heard the shots."

"He should've known someone would hear."

"They called nine-one-one. The police came."

"You testified against him? He went to jail?"

"Yes. But it's not over. Every night, when I go to bed and close my eyes, I see him in my mind."

She started to cry, forehead on her knees, arms still wrapped around her legs.

I slipped my arm around her and held her. I would have liked to hear more. Did her parents kick her out of the house? Is that why she was living with Tom and Elaine? If her father disapproved of Logan, why was he paying for daycare? Did she leave home to escape the stigma of rape?

"Don't cry," I said.

"Sorry I'm being such a baby about this."

She reached into the back pocket of her jeans for a tissue and wiped her eyes and nose.

"I think you're brave."

As she lifted her face toward mine, her eyes were soft and teary, full of mystery. I felt heat rising from her face and smelled perfume in her hair. Was she giving me consent to really kiss her?

How far could I go?

I never had any doubt with Mindy. From the first night we met, all the way was the only way.

Robyn's arm circled my neck, drawing me close.

I kissed her. Her lips parted, hesitantly. She trembled everywhere, and then my heart seemed to stumble.

I stopped.

I felt clumsy, my lips thick.

I never had to go slowly with Mindy. Never had to wonder about her feelings. I needed only to satisfy my own urges, and Mindy would somehow find her own satisfaction. But this girl had been raped. I sensed this was her first intimate moment with a boy since then. She was scared. Fragile. Vulnerable. Somehow—don't ask me how—I realize she needed to be treated with delicacy. She was not someone I wanted to bang for a moment's thrill. *Wham! Bam! Thank you, ma'am!*

And suddenly, despite all my experience with Mindy, I felt inexperienced.

Robyn said, "What's wrong?"

My throat seemed clogged. "It's nothing. I was just thinking. I mean, honestly, I was . . . about what happened to you."

She gave a little nod. "It's funny how an experience like that affects not only the victim but also everyone else who knows about it."

"Maybe if I just hold you, is that all right?"

"That'll be perfect."

She fell asleep in my arms, her breathing heavy and rhythmic. I fell asleep, too. A grandfather clock's *bong! bong! bonging!* at eleven from somewhere in the house woke me. Robyn was warm and comfortable in my arms, but I knew it would be wise for me to split before Tom and Elaine came home and found us like this.

Shaking Robyn gently by the shoulder, I woke her and said, "I have to take off."

She yawned. Rubbed her eyes, like a little girl. "What time is it?"

"Eleven."

"Yes, you'd better go."

"I had a great day," I said.

"Me, too." Her arms stretched in a long-sleeved shirt, and she yawned.

"Can I see you tomorrow?" I smiled at her. *"May* I?"

"If you want to," she said.

"I want to."

My eyes focused on her lips, and I felt myself turning warm inside. I wanted to kiss her again, but I was afraid she'd think I was trying to start something before I left, but I wasn't. Really, I was thinking it was remarkable that after what she'd been through, she trusted me this far. I mean, to be alone with her in my arms in the dark. Cool.

I left at eleven-thirty, never having touched her. Well, just a few kisses. And you can't imagine how great I felt about myself for having shown some restraint, but how confused I still was. If Robyn's ex-boyfriend was into drugs, I'll bet Robyn had been, too. But she seemed clean now.

Was Alan Blythwood still in jail? Must be. Rape is a serious crime. He got five to ten years, probably. Maybe he was doing more time for possession of drugs.

Or was he out? Was she hiding from him?

As I turned the key and started my truck, I was wondering how much more there was to know about Robyn Knight.

nineteen

I woke at nine in the morning to the jangle of the tele-phone downstairs in the kitchen. I popped out of bed and raced down the stairs in my jockey shorts, stubbing my big toe on the doorjamb, swearing. I jerked the phone to my ear. No one called my folks or me on a Sunday morning. I couldn't imagine who this might be.

Mindy? Maybe she wanted to come home. She wanted me to rescue her.

"Hello?"

"Stony," Robyn said, "I have to talk to you. Not on the phone, though."

"Hey," I said. "How are you? Did you dream of bobbers bobbing in the river last night?"

"I need to see you."

"What's wrong?"

"I can't explain it right now."

"You want me to call back later?"

"No," she said. "Don't call my sister's house. Don't come by. Meet me at the Hy-Vee on Rockingham. One o'clock. You know where it is?"

"You want to meet at a supermarket?"

"In the cafeteria part."

"All right," I said. "What's wrong?"

Click!

She hung up.

I stood there, staring at the phone in my hand.

I knew the worst had happened.

Her sister and husband probably thought I stayed too late last night. They thought the worst of me. When she told them I was a hick from Hickory Ridge, they forbid her to see me or talk to me. For her sake. And Logan's. If she wanted to live at their house, she had to live by their rules.

I slammed the receiver into its cradle in the wall.

The bathroom door—we have a bathroom right off the kitchen—opened and Dad stood in the doorway, looking baggy-eyed and hung over. He was dressed in his jeans, no shirt, no shoes.

His sudden appearance surprised me.

"What was that all about, this early in the morning?" Dad rubbed his stubbled beard. Scratched his hairy chest.

I shrugged. "Just a girl."

"Mindy?"

"A different girl."

"Get dressed. I'll make breakfast. Mom's working."

While showering in our upstairs bathroom, I debated about telling Dad our house had been spray painted again, the same symbol, probably the work of a prankster. But by the time I was dressed and came back downstairs, I decided not to.

One other thing. Before I left the bathroom, I felt around the back of my head for the little pigtail Mindy liked so much and insisted that I wear. But she was no longer a player in my life, and I needed to keep looking forward—so I grabbed a razor, sliced off my pigtail and beads, and flushed them.

Dad had made his morning cocktail and was frying bacon and eggs. The aroma filled my nostrils, awakening my hunger.

At the table while we ate, I told him I broke up with Mindy. She'd found a new boyfriend and I'd found a new girlfriend, though I wasn't quite sure of my status with her.

"A new girlfriend?" Dad cleared the last of the egg yoke off his plate with a swipe of toast.

"Just a girl I met at school. A really nice girl. Smart."

"What's her name?"

"Robyn Knight. She's been helping me with American Lit. So I can stay eligible for football."

"Got to stay eligible," Dad said. "I had trouble like that, too." Then he thought a moment and said, "I like Mindy. Where'd you say she went to?"

"Missouri."

"She reminds me a lot of your mom when she was young. A bit reckless. Headstrong."

I nodded silently, realizing if Mindy and I had married, we probably would have ended up exactly like my mom and dad. Is that what I wanted? Why not? I could probably find another girl wired like Mindy, marry her, stay here. No hassle. Maybe I could chase after Mindy. Break Eric Small's face. Win Mindy back.

Dad sipped his cocktail. "Been thinking we should start painting the whole house soon."

I nodded. "Sure. Whenever you want to start."

He shoved his chair back from the table and dumped his plate in the sink. That was different. He usually left it on the table.

When he took his beer into the living room to watch his Sunday morning fishing show on TV, I slipped outside to inspect the side of our house and blew out a big sigh. No new heart, dripping blood, thank God. And the image I painted over the other night hadn't bled through. Good.

Hands on my hips, I peered up at the many-limbed oak tree on our corner, a cloudy, threatening sky above it. Half of its autum-brown leaves were gone. I had to find the painter before Dad and I painted the house. My folks would be totally pissed if the spray painter struck after Dad and I slapped fresh paint on the place.

Maybe tonight I needed to climb that tree—I'd climbed it a million times when I was a kid. Wouldn't the painter be surprised when I leaped down and kicked the hell out of him. Or her.

· · ·

I sat across from Robyn in a booth at the Hy-Vee grocery store cafeteria, inhaling its greasy smells of hamburger, sausage, ham, and French fries. I tried to buy her something to eat, but she refused. I bought a Coke for each of us, anyway.

Tom and Elaine had taken Logan to the mall.

A few gray-haired senior citizens sat in booths, sipping coffee, studying their grocery lists through the bottom of their glasses, some of them smoking cigarettes in a restricted area.

Robyn twisted a turquoise ring around and around on her thumb and repeated, "I can't see you again, Stony."

I expected her rejection, but still it was a jolt. Like being called offside in a football game and getting slapped with a hundred-yard penalty.

"Give me one good reason," I said.

Robyn anchored her hair on the right side behind her ear. "When I was young, I was in a lot of trouble, hanging out with Alan—I'm sure you realize that."

"So you made a mistake. We all do."

"I was blind. I didn't understand what a loser he was. He was very abusive."

"I already know that—a guy who would rape a girl at gunpoint is obviously abusive."

"He was rich. But I didn't care about his money. My parents have money, too." Her voice sounded a little tight now. Uneven.

"He play sports?"

"Not at all. It was—I don't know. His good looks, his bad-boy reputation, his tattoos—the second I saw him I wanted him. He fascinated me."

I rolled my eyes. I couldn't believe a girl could like a guy who beat her up.

"He looked young," she said. "Little boyish almost—smooth skin and bright blue eyes that sometimes radiated innocence."

"You sound as if you're still in love with him."

"Absolutely not! Sometimes I hate him. Sometimes I feel sorry for him—his real weakness was he played with drugs and didn't know when was enough."

I leaned back in my booth. "You did drugs with him?"

"I never did. But I thought if I loved him enough—if he loved me—I could fix him."

"Didn't work, did it?"

"In the beginning," she said, "I thought it was." She wrapped her hands tight around her glass of Coke. "Like everything was playful. He'd throw me on the bed. Tickle me. Pinch me. Sometimes punch me on the arm. Wrestle with me and twist my arm. Bend my fingers."

"How long did the fun last?"

"Not long enough. Soon he was hitting me because I was wearing my hair up—he wanted it down that day. Or because I wore too much makeup. Or not enough. My skirt was too short. Too long. Then sometimes he wanted me to wear no underwear. He wanted complete control over my life."

"You didn't tell anyone?"

"I was too ashamed. I made excuses for my bruises—they always happened because of gymnastics."

"Didn't your parents suspect something?"

"They worked a lot. And late. They had no idea. Until I got pregnant."

"The tattoo?"

"My parents were furious about the tattoos, but I didn't tell them the tattoos were Alan's idea. I wanted them to like Alan."

"So you stayed with this guy?"

"I loved him, Stony." Her fingers clenched, unclenched around her glass. "He gave me black eyes and bruises, but he'd always cry later, say he was sorry, and beg me to forgive him."

"He conned you."

"Making up was wonderful. He was gentle, kind, passionate."

"But he was using you for a punching bag, Robyn."

"I felt I was the only one who understood him. He needed me."

I slid my glass from hand to hand. "It's a wonder he didn't kill you."

She nodded. "When I got pregnant, I started to think about the future and the kind of life I wanted to have for my baby. A life without violence. Alan wanted me to get an abortion—everything about him was about controlling me. A baby would interfere."

"He's why you dropped gymnastics, isn't it?"

"Yes, I gave up gymnastics for him, but I wouldn't give up my baby. Still, he insisted. 'I don't want a damn kid,' he said, and I suddenly stopped hoping I could fix him—I realized if his baby couldn't change him, nothing could. I didn't love him anymore."

She stopped, stared at her Coke, then drank through the straw.

"Wait a minute," I said slowly. "Do I remind you of him because I'm a football player—therefore violent?"

She waggled her head. "No, no, no. Just listen to me."

"All right."

"Alan was seventeen when they put him away—I told you that. The court tried him as a juvenile. He got out when he was eighteen. A year ago, and he—"

But I couldn't just listen.

"He broke into your house," I said. "He had a gun. He raped you. He was doing drugs. That's all he got? A year?"

"He was tried as a juvenile, I'm telling you. He had no prior record. He said he didn't threaten me with the gun. He just shot in the air. Never pointed it at me. All the holes were in the ceiling. He said he didn't rape me. He said I participated willingly."

I kept shaking my head in disbelief. "They let him out?"

"Prisons are desperately overcrowded these days."

"That's why you're living here?" I said. "So he won't find you?"

"My parents decided to move me just before he got out last year. This was my only place to go. With Tom and Elaine."

"And now he's looking for you?"

"I don't know. That's the worst part. We both could be in great danger—you and me. Logan, too. Alan promised revenge. His final words to me were, 'I'll get even, bitch.'"

I sat there frowning, trying to grasp everything she'd told me.

She said, "Do you know what we almost did last night?"

I puffed out a long breath. "Yes. But I wasn't going to hurt you. Or make you do anything you didn't want to."

"I know that."

"I never would. Honest."

"I believe you." She dabbed at her hazel eyes with a napkin. "I really, really like you, Stony, but I can't get involved with anyone like that just now. I've got too much to do. Too much responsibility. I mean, I have to show Logan how to live his life right."

"So your decision again is to blow me off. This time for good."

She gave her plastic glass a sharp rap off the table. "I have to—I don't want to."

"We couldn't simply be friends?"

"Do you think that would honestly work?"

I shrugged. "I don't know. Probably not."

"Want to see another tattoo?"

"Sure," I said. "Show them all to me."

"This is a tattoo Alan and I each got soon after we first met. I was desperate to be with him every minute—terrified of being alone. I thought I couldn't live without him. The tattoo united us."

Slowly Robyn unbuttoned the left cuff on her long-sleeved flannel shirt and hiked the sleeve up her arm. "Now it's my constant reminder of where I've been and where I don't want to go again." She flipped over her hand, exposing the inside of her wrist. "I'm so scared I won't get to college. Do something with my life. Provide for Logan. I have to stay focused."

The sight of the tattoo popped my eyes wide open, my stomach clenching.

"It's not pretty, is it?" Robyn said. "Alan has one on his right wrist. A symbol of our undying love."

I was stunned into silence. My whole world seemed to tilt, I was sliding off, but I couldn't find anything to grab to save myself. Couldn't find my voice to scream for help.

My fingers trembled as I took her hand in mine and traced my finger around the blood-dripping red heart on her cool skin. Her pulse beating beneath it, the heart felt alive.

With my fingertip I touched each of the three drops of blood.

She said, "Horrible, right?"

"Worse than the dragon."

"The drops of blood mean Alan and I would rather die than be apart. One drop is his, one drop is mine, and the last drop is the devil's."

A sick feeling fluttered in my stomach. "That's weird."

"Alan turned out weird." She looked at me. "You're pale. Are you all right?

"I don't know." I could barely talk. "S-someone spray painted a heart like that on my house," I said. "Twice."

twenty

Robyn's head snapped up, her eyes wide. It was her turn to be stunned.

She said, "What?" A whisper.

"Last week," I said, "my house was spray painted twice. A heart dripping blood. Like on your wrist. But I've painted over it."

"You never said anything."

"Your house being spray painted isn't something you brag about."

She drew a shuddering breath.

"You don't think . . . ?" I started, but what I was about to suggest seemed too incredible.

"I have to go," Robyn said, and shoved her Coke aside.

"You think it's Alan who spray painted my house? He's here?"

She gave my hand a squeeze. "It's him. A warning. He likes to play games. And he's my worst fear."

Sliding out of the booth, Robyn snatched her floppy hat from the hook above her seat and strode toward the door leading to the parking lot.

I followed, catching her as the automatic glass doors slid open.

"What are you going to do?" I said.

Outside, the air was chilly, the sky a dull gray, heavy clouds scudding by. An old man pushed an empty grocery cart past us toward the store.

Robyn took off across the parking lot, clamping her floppy hat to the top of her head with her hand.

"Wait a minute!" I caught her again and grabbed her arm, halting her. "What are you going to do?"

"Get home as soon as I can. Tell Tom and Elaine we have to be on an even more careful watch. Call my dad. Have him call the police at home. See if they have any word about Alan's whereabouts. If he's been spotted recently at home. Picked up for anything."

She took off for the corner of the parking lot, dodging a grizzled old guy hauling a huge garbage sack of empty aluminum cans over his shoulder to the store. I nearly bowled the guy over.

I suddenly realized something that now seemed very obvious. If Alan spray painted my house, that meant the guy had been following Robyn and me. Stalking us.

My head swiveled, as I tried to take in every car, every person in the parking lot at once. But I didn't know who I was looking for. Height. Size. Shape. Hair. I didn't know anything for sure about Alan Blythwood. Except that he was a creep. A druggie. An abuser.

Robyn stopped at a new yellow PT Cruiser and stabbed a key into the lock.

I said, "Have you got a picture of him? I'm in this, too, you know. He might be watching us right now. I'd like to know what he looks like. You could give a picture to the cops."

"Why would I keep a picture of him?"

"At least describe him to me a little better."

She swung the car door open. "Stony, I've got to get home."

"You're not in this alone. I've got a stake, too."

Standing on her tiptoes, holding the brim of her floppy hat up, she stretched and kissed me on the mouth, surprising me. "I'll call you."

She slipped into the car.

"When?"

"As soon as I can."

She closed the door and twisted the key in the ignition. The little yellow car purred to life. She locked her door and backed up.

I watched her zoom out of the parking lot. Other cars pulled out. Old people. All of them. No one seemed to be following her. How could I be sure?

Licking my lips, I still tasted her kiss. I was thinking I should follow her home to make sure Alan wasn't waiting for her, but if Tom and Elaine were there, the sight of me showing up would probably make them put more pressure on Robyn to keep me out of her life. I didn't want that.

. . .

I sat hunched on the front porch steps of my house with Mom.

It was 5:00 PM. Four long hours had gone by since Robyn left me in the Hy-Vee parking lot.

Never in my life had I been more confused, worried, frustrated. Alan was in town. He was stalking Robyn and me. How could I find him, somehow trap him, then turn him over to the cops?

But he hadn't done anything wrong. Only spray painted my house. And I had no real proof of that.

The day remained gray, chilly, and gloomy. Last night's wind and rain had beaten the colorful leaves off the trees. Soggy and matted, they cluttered the grass, sidewalk, and street.

Dad had walked down to the bait shop to take over for Mom. Give her a break. I couldn't remember the last time he'd done that for Mom on a Sunday. I'd been telling Mom about my breakup with Mindy and about the new girl in my life. The stuff about Alan I left out, though. I'd been able to convince Mom that the heart spray painted on our house was the work of some unknown prankster, a one-time thing.

"I always worried about you when you were out with Mindy," Mom said. "Had a feeling she'd get you in trouble." Mom gave me a tiny smile. "You know what I mean?"

"I know."

Mom sighed and leaned back against the porch railing. "Seems like kids are having such a terrible time these days. In my day, we just had fun. Drank a little beer. Smoked cigarettes. Some did drugs. But not like these days."

I drummed my fingers on the porch steps. I wasn't worried about what was happening to kids these days. I was wondering, *Will Robyn really call?*

I remembered distinctly she'd said, *I'll call you . . . as soon as I can.*

From where I sat on the front porch with the door open, I was sure I could hear the telephone, but it hadn't rung once since I'd gotten home from Hy-Vee. I wished I had the cordless in my lap right now, but it was dead. It needed a new battery.

To somehow find and trap Alan Blythwood, I at least needed to know what the creep looked like.

I pictured him as being skinny, slimy, sneaky—a snake.

A crow hopped across the street and pecked at road-kill, a red squirrel.

Mom said, "I think Dad's working the bait shop today because he thinks if he helps a little I won't sell it—maybe I won't if he stays out of the tavern. Always thought you might help more."

"I'm sorry," I said. "I know I should."

"I mean after you graduate and go to work in the quarry, you might have more time. We could be like partners, maybe."

"That would probably work but—" I'd been about to surprise myself—Mom, too, I'm sure—and say, *I think I might go to college*. But I stopped, took a tiny breath, and wiped my sweaty palms on my jeans.

I mean, when I thought about what had happened to Robyn, and I saw how hard she was fighting back, so determined, and how I was sitting around doing nothing, my thumb stuck up my ass, I felt like a worthless lump of flesh—a guy who was wasting his life smiling too much.

Mindy was probably wasting her life, but at least she'd made a decision about which way she wanted to go. Brian had made some bad choices, but he was back on track.

Me? I hadn't made choices of any kind. Good or bad.

Except pass American Lit. Play tough football.

I gulped and said, "I might go to college."

Saying that was so scary I shivered. The thought made me feel suddenly lost, like I was cast adrift on an inner tube, riding a treacherous current down the Mississippi headed for where I didn't know, the security of home left behind me. No safety net at all.

Mom clasped her hands in front of her and stared at me. "Get out of here! No Stoneking's gone to college. Not that I heard of. No one on my side of the family, either. All my kin have been hard-working Iowa farmers, hardly a penny to their name but honest."

"I'm going to try, I think."

"You haven't got the grades. Your counselor is always calling here. Telling me you're failing."

"I'm going to try really hard this year," I said, and my chest puffed a little. "Maybe get As in all my classes. And if our football team does well, and if I play well, maybe I can get a scholarship."

"Lord, you're serious, aren't you?"

"I am, Mom. I really am. It's a choice I'm going to make."

She smiled at me. A big, round smile with lots of wrinkles around the corners of her eyes and mouth.

"Well, I hope you do!" She slapped her knee. "It's time a Stoneking got out of that quarry and done something with their life."

Rrring!

I heard the sharp sound of the phone and leaped up.

"I'll get it!"

I answered in the kitchen on the third ring.

"Robyn—?" I said, breathless.

"Stony"—it was Dad—"ask your mom how late she thinks I should stay open. Nobody's been by in the past hour, weather cloudy and bad as it is."

"I'll get her." I slammed out the front door. "Mom, Dad wants to talk to you. But don't be too long. I—"

That's when I spotted a yellow PT Cruiser wheeling around the corner and skidding to a stop in front of my house.

twenty-one

Robyn jumped out of the car, marched across the lawn and sidewalk, and stopped at the bottom of the porch steps. Before she said a word, I felt chilled. It was the way she looked. Rigid and pale. Fists clenched at her sides. Lips quivering.

"You've got to help me." Her voice was quivering, too.

"What is it?"

"Can we be someplace alone?"

"Backyard. A picnic table. Is that all right?"

She nodded. "Show me the graffiti on your house."

"I painted over it, I told you."

"Show me."

I clutched her hand, and we hurried around to the side of the house.

I said, "See. It didn't even bleed through."

"The heart was just like on my wrist? Three drops of blood?"

"Yes. He's really here, isn't he?" It was a stupid question, and my own heart was suddenly beating a hundred points faster.

She nodded. "I just talked to him." She started shaking all over. "Can we sit down?"

I led her to the backyard where we sat across from each other on a picnic table under a huge willow tree. The sky was still gray and threatening.

"You saw him?" I said. "Or he called?"

"He called." Tears flooded Robyn's eyes. "He's kidnapped Logan."

Cold fear stabbed me, and goose bumps popped up on my arms, across my neck and shoulders.

"Kidnapped? How?" *This can't be true!* "When?"

"At the mall." She was talking rapidly now, the words tumbling out, as she wiped the tears from her eyes with her fingertips. "He followed them to the mall, Tom and Elaine and Logan. My sister and her husband were looking at winter coats for Logan. Tom thought Elaine had a hold of Logan's hand. Elaine thought Tom had him. Logan must've wandered away."

I nodded. "Something probably caught his eye."

Robyn pounded the table with a doubled fist. "We've told him a million times always to stay close to us. Never go with a stranger."

I grabbed her hand before she pounded the table again and hurt herself. "It's hard to hang on to a kid every second. I could never keep track of Shane."

"By the time Tom and Elaine realized neither one of them held his hand, he'd vanished."

"No cry from Logan? No struggle? Didn't anybody see anything?"

"Parents are always struggling with their kids at the mall. Dragging them along by an arm, the kid crying. The police have already talked to dozens of people, both employees and shoppers who were there. No one saw anything unusual."

"How did you find out?" I reached across the table, taking both her hands now, lacing my fingers with hers.

"When I got home from Hy-Vee, that's when Alan called. Logan told him the number. He said he'd been calling every five minutes. He finally got me. Tom and Elaine were already at the police station, making a statement. Then they called, and I went straight to the station. They're going crazy. I just came from the police."

"What does the creep want? Money? What?"

"Me. Tonight."

I stared at her in amazement.

"In exchange for Logan," she said.

My skin prickled.

Mom came out the back door and across the lawn. Robyn and I dropped our hands to our laps.

"I wondered what happened to you," Mom said to me, while smiling at Robyn. "Hello, I'm Wendell's mother."

As I introduced her, Robyn quickly tried to wipe more tears away from her eyes with her sleeve. "This is Robyn, Mom. She's been helping me with my American Lit."

"Hello, Mrs. Stoneking," Robyn said.

"Is something wrong?" Mom said.

"Mom, it's nothing," I said. "Really."

"You're sure?"

"Positive, Mom. Please . . ."

Mom nodded. "I'm going down to the bait shop. Help your dad close. You're sure everything's all right?"

"We'll be fine, Mom."

I watched Mom hustle down the sidewalk dressed in old jeans and sweatshirt, then turned to Robyn and gripped both her hands again across the picnic table, rubbing my thumbs over her knuckles.

I said, "You told the police Alan called, didn't you? That he's here. Told them what he wants."

Robyn shook her head. "If I tell the police, he'll kill Logan. He told me he would. I know he'll do it."

"The bastard's crazy."

"But my sister told the police about Alan. She's positive Alan kidnapped Logan. The police aren't sure. They're talking to the cops at home, trying to find out if he's still in that area."

"At least you pulled Tom and Elaine aside and told them about talking to Alan and what he wants, didn't you?"

"I haven't told them anything." Robyn lowered her eyes.

I threw my head back a second and studied the tangle of drooping willow branches above me. "Am I hearing right? Tom and Elaine don't know the guy called? That he's here? The police don't know?"

"That's right."

"So Tom and Elaine are sitting home going crazy with guilt. Not knowing anything about Logan. Wondering what's up. And you're planning a swap, yourself for Logan?"

"And I need your help, Stony."

I released Robyn's hands and sat up straight. My gaze hit her straight in her hazel eyes. "My help, how?"

"Alan said he'd give Logan back at midnight. I need you to take him home to Tom and Elaine."

"I don't believe this."

"It'll work. Logan likes you. Trusts you. He'll go with you. It's the only way."

"What happens to you?"

"I go with Alan. I'll be all right."

"No way!" I jumped up from the table and stood over her. "You've got to tell the police. That's the *only* way."

She shook her head, her eyes swimming in tears now. "I won't!"

"Where does this exchange go down?"

"An abandoned hotel building on the east edge of town. I have an address. Will you help me find it tonight?"

"Tell me again exactly what happens to you after the exchange."

"I told you—I go with Alan. After you take Logan home, call the police, and they can start looking for us. Alan might even take me back home."

"The police would probably throw me in jail for helping you with such a stupid plan. They might find you dead in a ditch someplace. Ever think of that?"

"It won't work unless I have someone to take Logan."

I inhaled, exhaled.

Robyn said, "We meet in this abandoned building at midnight. Fourth floor. First room on the right at the top of the stairs. No cops. No guns. No flashlights. We make the exchange in the room."

"Will Alan be alone?"

"I don't know. He didn't say, I didn't ask. He said I could bring one person. You."

I frowned. "He specifically asked for me?"

"Yes."

"Why me?"

"I don't know."

I rubbed my forehead, trying to think. *Why me?* I said, "I can't imagine he'd attempt this by himself. Why not make the exchange in a dark alley somewhere? From car to car."

"I don't know."

I leaned on the picnic table. "Let's tell the police."

"You want Logan dead? Alan will kill him, I'm telling you!" Robyn stared at me, eyeball to eyeball. "Wouldn't you do the same thing for your brother Shane if you had to?"

My shoulders slumped. I hated her plan. Positively hated it.

I could refuse her, then go to the police myself with the story. Tell them everything.

But the result might be Logan's death.

I couldn't chance it.

"All right," I said. "Where is this abandoned building?"

. . .

We drove in my mom's old silver Buick Century. I was sure if Alan was anywhere near the abandoned building when we arrived, the creep would recognize my truck. I mean, he'd obviously been stalking us—he'd seen the truck before. He probably followed us to Wildcat Den. That prompted the spray paintings on my house. He probably watched us take off to go fishing and waited until we came back. He probably leered through a window last night as Robyn and I kissed in her sister's house. That prompted the kidnapping.

Robyn said, "Are you sure this is the right thing to do, driving by? What if he sees us and calls the whole thing off?"

"Good."

"I'm serious."

"Look," I said. "I'm not sure either of us is going into that building tonight. But if we do, I want to get a good look at it from the outside. I want to see where we can run to if we get out—I'm not going to let you go with him."

"You have to."

"Not if I can help it."

We found the building on a corner on the outskirts of the old part of downtown.

Crossing railroad tracks, I drove slowly by the front of it.

It was a huge, abandoned, four-story, brick building—the Standard Hotel. I guessed there might have once been twenty or thirty units in the building, perhaps a prestigious, ritzy place to stay fifty, sixty years, seventy years ago.

Now graffiti of all kinds decorated the walls: stars, crowns, Playboy bunnies, champagne glasses, hearts, snakes, spiders, initials, several skulls and crossbones. The two doors in front of the building and all the windows on the first two floors were boarded up. The windows on the upper floors either gaped blindly down at the street or were broken out. Hundreds of pigeons roosted on the window ledges or strutted on the roof's cornice.

The thought of entering the building at midnight, without a flashlight—even with a flashlight—sent a chill up my spine.

"How do we get in?" I said.

"A fire escape exit door along the side of the building."

"We'd have to be crazy to go in there," I said. "The police station's downtown. Ten or fifteen blocks from here. Let's talk to the cops."

"I'm going in at midnight," Robyn said. "With or without you."

"Then what do you think will happen?"

"I'll convince Alan to take Logan home before he takes me wherever he's going to take me."

He'll throw Logan out a fourth-floor window!

"Fat chance he'll do that," I said.

Next to the hotel sat a white cement-block building whose signs advertised body and fender work and car painting. Cheap. A twelve-foot-high chain-link fence surrounded the building, and a huge parking lot with a few junky-looking cars occupied the rest of the block.

I circled the block and came up along the side of the hotel. The side street was very wide and paved with brick. Railroad tracks ran through the center of the street. In back of the hotel, facing the brick street and railroad tracks, was another empty hulk of a building, abandoned and boarded up. It had once been a bar and restaurant. A dirty, faded, barely readable sign running the length of the building still proclaimed DEMPSEY'S FINE FOODS AND SPIRITS.

The side of the Standard Hotel looked like the front. Graffiti spray painted everywhere. Windows boarded or broken. Pigeons roosting, strutting.

I said, "Where's the fire-exit door we're supposed to use?"

"The tiny walk space between the hotel and that empty restaurant. That's where the door is."

As we drove slowly by, I glanced down the walk space. The area was littered with broken glass, newspapers, and a car tire. "I don't see anyplace to hide around here, if we had to."

"Let's leave," Robyn said. "We've seen everything."

I agreed. I'd seen enough to know the idea of swapping her for Logan in that abandoned hotel was stupid. Any kind of a swap anywhere was stupid. But what else could we do? What else could *I* do?

I punched the accelerator, turned right, and sped away.

What if I helped Robyn but secretly told the cops about the swap? The cops could move in and surround the building. Then after Logan and I escaped, they could capture Alan Blythwood as he tried to sneak away with Robyn. Or, if they had to, blow him away.

But what if Alan held a gun to Robyn's head and killed her before the cops could capture or kill him?

"It's all right," Robyn said. "You don't have to go with me. I understand how you feel. After I go home, please don't call the police, though."

Funny how she knew what I was thinking.

"Can I trust you?" she said.

"I can't believe this is going to be as simple as you think."

"Give me a chance to solve this my way. Please, Stony."

Dusk invaded the city. The lights of oncoming cars stared me in the eye. I switched my lights on and glanced at Robyn. She was watching me closely, waiting for my reply.

Mr. Duval had told me life was about setting goals and making smart choices. That was easy enough to say, but in some cases how do you tell if a choice is smart or stupid? Should you pass or run the ball? Coach Maddox faced that question all the time.

Maybe sometimes you have to go with your gut feeling.

I tightened my fingers on the steering wheel.

"I'll pick you up at eleven-thirty," I said. "A block from your house. On the corner."

"Thank you, thank you, Stony."

"Be careful sneaking out. You don't want to wake Tom or Elaine."

She leaned over and kissed me—I should have been thrilled—but I was wondering if someone was going to die tonight.

twenty-two

"You weren't supposed to bring a flashlight," Robyn whispered, as we felt our way along the walkway between the Standard Hotel and Dempsey's Fine Foods and Spirits. She was following me in the midnight darkness, grasping my sweaty hand.

"I've got it," I said, "and I'm going to use it."

Neither moon nor stars lit our way as we crunched along on broken glass.

I flashed my penlight over the hotel's brick wall, looking for the fire-exit door.

My blood hammered in my temples.

The night chilled me, and the walkway smelled of cat pee. Slashing the darkness, my penlight's beam finally spotted a closed rusty metal door. Handleless.

"This must be it," I said. "Did Alan say it would be open?"

"Pull on it." Robyn's breathing was quick and ragged.

I felt along the door's edge, seeking a place to pry it open. The steel was cold to my touch. My fingers found a spot where someone had pried at the door with a crowbar or something. The door's edge was buckled and bent enough for my fingers to hook it.

"Take this," I said and gave the light to Robyn.

With the fingers of both hands I pulled, and the door creaked open, swinging out.

Bracing myself, I took a deep breath.

"This must be it," I said. "Want to change your mind?"

"No," Robyn said. "Logan's up there."

She handed me the flashlight, grabbed my hand, and we stepped cautiously into the building, leaving the door open. Inside, I stood still, listening carefully, holding my breath a moment.

Squeak! Squeak! Squeak!

A rat! Its high-pitched, panicky squeal cut the silence, and I jumped back as the varmint scrambled across my Nikes.

Robyn stifled a scream with a fist at her mouth and shivered. "What was that?"

"Rats," I said. "Four-legged variety."

"Oh, my God . . ."

My light picked out the stairs near the exit. I took another deep breath. "Ready?"

"Yes." Barely audible.

"I hope we know what we're doing."

Shining the light on the worn wooden stairs, I ascended slowly, my back against the wall, Robyn following, her hand still clutching mine. Nearly every stair creaked. Cockroaches slithered about, and the air smelled sour—like dung or dead things—mice, rats, pigeons, bats. Humans? The thought wrenched my stomach. Litter cluttered the stairs: beer and wine bottles, wrappers and bags from fast food places. Cans. An old shoe. Transients apparently called this place home sometimes.

When we reached the second floor, we stopped.

My knees were shaking, and I felt Robyn trembling next to me.

"Let's keep going," she said, sounding brave. "Two more floors."

Man, she had guts. "All right."

Slowly we felt our way up the second flight of stairs. Felt our way along the rough, plastered walls.

Creak! Creak! Creak!

Every step made a sound.

Third floor. Because of the broken windows—no ply-wood boards nailed over them—cold air rushed down the hallway. Shivering, I flicked off my light and stuck it in my jeans jacket pocket. Tomb-like darkness enveloped us.

I gulped. "I think we can make the rest of the way in the dark, don't you?"

"Yes." Robyn's voice shook.

Feeling my way along the wall, I stumbled on the first step. Robyn crashed into me, and we both held our breath. "Sorry," I said.

Climbing this last flight of stairs in the dark seemed to take forever, but finally we creaked our way to the top and stood on the fourth-floor landing, both of us trembling, and I heard only the quick sound of our breathing. The intense, suffocating darkness pushed in on us from all sides.

First room to the right.

My eyes strained in the darkness, but I couldn't see where the room was or if the door was open or not.

"To hell with this," I said under my breath, and reached in my jacket pocket for my penlight. But suddenly I sensed a third presence nearby, and the muscles in my back twitched a warning.

I tensed. Stopped breathing.

A voice from out of the darkness in front of me said, "This way, dudes. It's all good."

The skin on my face tightened.

Suddenly a blinding light hit me in the face. Remained in my face. A second light must have hit Robyn in the face, too, because she gave a startled gasp, and I tasted fear for the first time in my life. It was the taste of lead in my mouth, a sinker for pan fishing.

I wondered if I would pee my pants.

When I tried to tilt my head away from the light, the voice said, "Face this way, dude. Walk forward. I got Blacky pointed straight at you."

"Blacky?" I asked.

"Trey-eight, dude. Automatic!"

The voice was high-pitched. Like a young teen's. A trey-eight must have been a thirty-eight caliber gun.

Squinting in the light, turning my head slightly aside, I shuffled forward, Robyn alongside of me, a light still in her eyes, too. The room smelled of beer. And weed.

"How you been, sweetness?"

"Alan?" Robyn said. "With this light in my face, I can't see anything."

"I'm your man," the voice said. "Come to rescue you."

"Where's Logan?" Robyn said. "I want to see him."

"No problem," Alan said. "Mud, my man, put the light on him."

The beams of light on Robyn's and my faces suddenly dropped off us and splashed on Logan as he stood motionless in front of Mud's legs and feet. Mud made no sound as he gripped Logan's hand. A piece of silver duct tape covered the boy's mouth, and in the bright light his eyes shone wild and glassy with terror. I spotted two empty Colt 45 beer bottles on the floor at Mud's feet.

Logan tried to yank and pry his hand free from Mud's grasp, but Mud only gripped him harder.

"You bastard!" Robyn said.

A light hit me again in the face, blinding me, and Robyn said, "Take that tape off! Let him go. Get that light out of my eyes." Her voice no longer shook with fear. It vibrated with rage.

"When ready," Alan said. "First we're going to party, sweetness, me and you."

"Like hell!" Robyn said.

As my mind churned, assessing the situation, I suddenly felt my own rage pumping through my veins. Only two of them. With flashlights. Alan with a gun. Mud—a street name, probably—might have a gun, too, but right now both his hands were busy. One gripped a flashlight. The other, Logan's hand.

Keep them talking. Delay the swap. Like in football. Hang in there. Make something happen. Piss them off. Force a fumble.

"You the creep who spray painted my house?" I asked, and blinked rapidly because of the blinding light in my eyes. Slowly the light divided in two, as if a flashlight was shining in each eye, the one in the left eye much brighter.

"You be messin' with my woman," Alan said. "You understand what I'm saying? Artwork on your house gives you something to think about, dude. Right?" The shaft of light suddenly dipped from my face. Slid over my body, searching. "You carrying?"

"No," I said.

"Drop the jacket."

I shrugged out of my jeans jacket, and it tumbled to the floor. "Satisfied?"

"Turn around."

I turned completely around, and the light struck me in the face again. My eyes were starting to burn, but I kept them open. "Satisfied?"

"It's all good," Alan said.

"How did you find me?" Robyn said.

"Took a long time, sweetness. Every night searching your daddy's garbage for an envelope. A card. Something with a name and address on it. I knew you had a sister somewhere."

"Let Logan go with Stony," Robyn said. "I'll go with you. Like we agreed."

"You tell the dude about us?" Alan said. "How we made mad, passionate love night and day? How you belong to only me?"

"She doesn't *belong* to anybody," I said.

"Stony, please . . ." Robyn said.

Alan laughed, a nasty, evil, high-pitched bark.

I said, "You're a bottom-feeder, you know that, asshole? Terrorizing your own son."

A hush fell over the room, and I heard the blood pounding in my ears.

Maybe I'd gone too far. But I was hoping Alan would step up to me, try to pistol-whip me, and I could take him out.

I heard Mud shift nervously from foot to foot, and Alan chuckled softly.

"He doesn't mean that," Robyn whispered. "Let's make the swap. I'll go with you. Like we agreed," she repeated.

"I think the dude said what he means. He must be crazy, though. Talk to me like that. Blacky on him." Alan chuckled again. "He'll like the party. Be good for him to watch. Teach him respect."

The light in my eyes suddenly flicked away, leaving me with a bright green spot in front of each eye, unable to see anything for a second. Then I saw a ragged, stained mattress on the floor.

"For me and you, sweetness," Alan said. "We take care of business tonight."

"No!" Robyn said.

"Everyone gets to watch."

"Never!" Robyn screamed.

"Mud here, he's dumb as dirt and twice as ugly. He doesn't have a lady. Just likes to watch and do his thing."

My mouth dropped open when I realized what was going to happen, and I felt Robyn cringe next to me. Now Mud gave a little chuckle. I wondered if he was smart enough to talk.

"No way!" I said. "This isn't going down!"

"Wait 'n see, dude. She's good."

twenty-three

The light swung back and stabbed me in the eyes. I blinked. Squinted.

"You're crazy!" I said.

Robyn screamed, "I won't!"

"Got to," Alan said. "Only this time it'll be rape. Wasn't last time. I went to jail because my lady lied. She tell you that?"

"Alan, you had a gun!" Robyn said. "You were so high you don't remember."

"Listen!" Alan barked. "Check it out! I never broke in. Never hit you. Never pointed the gun at you. You hear what I'm saying? You think I don't remember?"

"You kept firing the gun in the air, demanding."

"I never forced you!" Alan said.

"You had a *gun!*"

"You knew I'd never off you."

"You would Logan! I pleaded for you to leave—if you remember anything, you must remember that."

"Tonight I do the deed I already did time for." Another chuckle. "Bubble Gum can watch. I want him to watch his momma. Queen of Sweetness."

"No!" Robyn said.

"Dude, too, he can watch. Then me and you book, sweetness."

"You really are a crazy bastard," I said. My anger was a living, breathing creature inside me now.

"I won't!" Robyn screamed,

"Cool," Alan said. "I like a struggle. Lots more fun."

This was worse than anything I could have imagined. Except for Robyn or Logan getting killed. Or both of them. And me, too. And who said this freak wouldn't kill us anyway? I could see no faces behind the lights. No bodies. Had no idea how big or strong these creeps were.

If Alan was busy with Robyn on the mattress—if Mud was too interested in what he was watching, doing his thing—maybe I could surprise Alan. Overpower him.

God, I couldn't let it go that far, Alan and Robyn on the mattress. In front of Logan.

"Here's Bubble Gum," Alan said. "You take him. Hold him so he can watch. Now I want you, sweetness. But you wait there till I give Blacky to Mud. Then you get naked. Slow. Like you always do."

Mud released Logan, and I heard the boy come stumbling across the wooden floor, accidentally kicking aside an empty Colt 45 bottle. Stepping in front of Robyn, I knelt on one knee to pick up Logan.

But instead, sucking in a deep breath, my heart ramming my ribcage, I snatched my jeans jacket off the floor, cried "DUCK!" and hurled the jacket at Alan, whirling it, blocking out the beam from his flashlight.

A shot rang out, filling the room with its roar and the smell of gunpowder.

I felt no pain. Had no sense of being hit with a bullet.

As I shoved Logan to the floor, I dove low and hard, catching Alan across the thighs with a crunching block. Blacky fired again, flooding the room with another deafening roar and a stronger gunpowder smell. I slammed Alan across the room with my best power block ever, crunching him against the wall, and landed a knee-shot to his groin.

Alan gasped and groaned. Under my weight, the creep felt like a skinny sophomore. Alan's flashlight dropped to the floor, went out, and something else clattered to the floor. Blacky.

"Robyn!" I cried. "You all right?"

"Yes!" Robyn's voice. Panting.

"Get Logan. Run!"

At that instant Mud's light found me and flashed in my eyes. I knew he must be carrying. A blade, at least, if not a gun.

But if Mud was packing a weapon, he had no chance to use it. *Crack!* I heard glass shatter. Heard Mud groan "*Agggg . . .*" Watched his light drop to the floor and blink out. Heard Mud crumble to his knees and topple over.

Robyn had crunched his skull with a Colt 45 beer bottle.

"Robyn! Logan!" I cried in the darkness.

"I'm all right!" Robyn said. Breathless.

"Where's Logan?"

"I've got him," Robyn said.

I felt through the inky blackness for both of them. Touched Robyn's hot, tear-wet face. Knelt and scooped up Logan. Felt the boy cold and trembling in my arms.

I whispered, "You're going to be okay, Catfish. It's me. Stony. Hang on."

Logan wrapped his arms around my neck.

Mud groaned in a corner of the room. I heard a rustling, as if Alan had rolled over and was crawling along the floor. Maybe he'd found the gun!

"Let's get out of here!" I said.

Grabbing Robyn's hand, clutching Logan in my right arm, I edged out of the room, scuffed along the hallway, until I found the edge of the steps, then started feeling my way down, my back sliding against the wall. I reached for my penlight, but realized I'd dropped the light into my jeans jacket pocket, and the stupid jacket lay somewhere in the room on the floor. Probably a bullet hole through it.

"You okay?" I whispered back to Robyn.

"Yes. Hurry!"

I halted on the second floor and glanced up the stairs. No light yet.

"Hurry," Robyn said.

"You're going to be okay," I whispered again to Logan. He squeezed my neck tighter.

I was thinking Logan had to be totally terrified. Would he ever forget this nightmare? I wished I could stop a minute and carefully peel the tape from the boy's mouth without hurting him. Let him cry. Let him scream out loud. But for now it was perhaps better that the brave little guy remained silent.

On the second floor landing, I stumbled over garbage of some kind, cussed, but kept my balance.

"You okay?" Robyn said, wringing my hand.

"Fine."

"Logan?"

"He's going to be fine."

It wasn't until we reached the bottom floor that I heard the thumping, scuffling, and shouting above us on the fourth-floor landing. Saw the zigzagging flashlight beams slicing the darkness.

Then two shots rang out from above us, and Alan screamed down the stairwell, "You can't get away! You understand what I'm saying? You can't hide!"

"Run for the truck!" I told Robyn. I pushed her ahead of me, out the still-open fire-exit door, on to the walkway between the buildings. "I'm right behind you!"

The night was black and cold, but I was feeling good because I knew that across the brick street and railroad tracks my truck sat, only forty yards away, pointed toward downtown. Toward escape. Toward the police station.

As we scrambled along the walkway, I felt for my keys in my jean jacket pocket and remembered again—this time with gut-sinking horror—I threw my jacket at Alan. *Were my keys in it?*

I stopped in a panic, and with a trembling hand I dug in my left front pocket of my pants.

Nothing!

Robyn said, "What's wrong?"

I shifted Logan to my left arm. Dug in my right front pocket.

Yes! Keys!

It wasn't until I reached the sidewalk and stood frozen alongside Robyn that I realized my keys weren't going to do me any good. A train was chugging by. Right in front of our faces. My truck was on the other side of the tracks!

In the confusion, excitement, and horror, I hadn't heard a train coming. A big-ass freight train, its wheels grinding against the steel rails, the cars swaying as if they might topple. I glanced ahead of it. It had just started huffing by. I could see three, maybe four engines. I could tell by its slow, easy rumble and the number of engines that the train might be sixty or seventy cars long, taking maybe five minutes to pass us.

Any second Alan and Mud would come bursting through the fire escape door. If we headed down the street, we would never be able to outrun them, not with my carrying Logan. And there was no place to hide.

"Jump the train!" I yelled at Robyn above the clatter.

"What?"

"Jump the train!"

"I can't!"

"You have to!" I shouted. "There's no time!"

"You and Logan?"

"We'll jump a car behind you. Ride all the way downtown to the levee where the gambling boat dock is. Jump off when I do."

"Logan—?"

"I can handle him."

I pushed Robyn onto the brick street. The train churned by us, dangerously close, only a foot away, the wind it created blew our hair. I smelled diesel fuel, steel, coal dust. The bricks in the street vibrated underneath my soles, sending a shiver through me.

"Run alongside," I said. "The street's level. Sprint ahead of the rung you jump for, time your jump, hang on, anchor your feet on the lowest rung. It's only going maybe four, five miles an hour. *Go!*"

I watched breathlessly as Robyn raced along the brick street, leaped for the train, caught the rung, hung on, anchored her feet, climbed to the top of the coal car.

I shifted Logan to my left arm. My heart was pounding like mad, and my skin was tingling with a rush of adrenaline.

"Hang on, Catfish!"

I made my leap with Logan clutched in my arm three coal cars after Robyn, just as Alan fired Blacky two times from the street, the bullets sailing harmlessly into the night.

twenty-four

Sergeant Barbara Spear sat behind her desk in the Thompsonville Police Department under the glare of inlaid ceiling lights. She was staring at Robyn and me, swiveling her chair side to side and tapping a pencil on her desk. She was not happy.

Robyn and I hunched in metal chairs in front of Spear's desk.

Spear was tall, maybe two hundred pounds but not fat. Her curly red hair, the color of rust, was cropped short.

"That's your story?" Spear said. "You hopped a train and rode it to the levee where the gambling boat docks? You jumped off and ran to the police station?"

Ten or fifteen desks filled the noisy room along with eight or nine other police officers. Some officers were interviewing people. Others were rushing around like ants. One was clicking away at a computer; another, talking on a telephone, waving his hand.

"That's it," I said.

"Can we go?" Robyn said. "I want to be with Logan." It was nearly 2:00 AM.

"I want to get my truck," I said. "Before someone trashes it. It's parked across from the old Standard Hotel."

We had already been at the station over an hour. Robyn called Tom and Elaine as soon as she and I staggered in here, Logan hunched on my shoulders. Furious with us, Tom and Elaine rushed down to the station, listened to our story, and then took Logan home.

Robyn and I each wore a tiny microphone, hooked to a tape recorder sitting on Spear's desk.

"I want to hear a few things one more time," Spear said.

I shifted in my hard metal chair. "Seems like we've told you everything a hundred times."

Ignoring me, Spear looked at Robyn. "You think Logan's abductor and your attacker is a kid named Alan Blythwood, your ex-boyfriend from your hometown? Is that right?"

Robyn nodded. "That's right."

Spear said, "You believe that he was seeking retaliation because you'd sent him to jail for rape?"

"Yes."

"But you weren't able to see his face tonight. You can only identify him by his voice."

"I'd know his voice anywhere," I said. "High-pitched. Like a kid's."

"It was him," Robyn said, and this time she showed Spear the heart tattoo on her wrist. "When you find him, you'll see he has the same tattoo. Right wrist."

I said, "He spray painted my house twice with the same symbol."

"But neither of you can identify him positively," Spear said.

"It was total darkness," I said. "We told you this. They had lights in our faces. I can identify his voice. Isn't that good enough?"

"You don't know the other person?"

I shook my head. Sighed deeply. Why was she making us repeat everything? "Alan called him Mud. That's all I know."

"Same here," Robyn said.

I shifted once more in my chair. "If you don't believe us, check out the Standard Hotel. Fourth floor. A room in back above a ground-floor fire-exit door. My truck's parked on the street by the tracks. In the room you'll find my jacket. Probably a bullet hole through it. Roach butts. Colt 45 bottles. Shell casings. Probably casings on the stairway, too." I drew a disgusted breath. "Can't we go? *May* we go? We've told you this stuff a million times."

Spear reached over and punched the tape recorder's OFF button. "Don't get impatient with me, Wendell." She pulled off the tiny microphone pinned to her lapel and dropped it on her desk. "I've got people at the scene right now. I expect a call any second. Then we'll see how your story stands up." She pointed at our microphones. "Take them off."

Robyn and I unpinned ours and set them on the desk.

Spear said, "If anybody's going to get impatient here, it's me. Why didn't you call the police, young lady? What you two did tonight was absolutely foolish!"

"Alan would've killed Logan." I said it before Robyn could.

"You could've gotten yourselves shot," Spear said. "Or killed by a train. Police matters are best left to the police."

Spear's face was nearly as red as her bushy hair.

"I had to risk it," Robyn said.

"The police would've taken care—" A male cop tapped Spear on the shoulder. "Captain wants you in his office."

She halted. "All right," she said to the cop. She stared at Robyn and me. "I'm not finished with either one of you yet. Withholding information is a criminal offense, you know."

"But—" Robyn started.

Spear shut her down. "If you'd have let the police handle this, the two suspects would be in custody now. Stalkers—obsessed people like Alan Blythwood—don't go away. He's still out there, a danger to everyone."

"I realize that," Robyn said softly.

"Now we've got to find him. He'd be in custody if you hadn't interfered. Think about that."

"Logan would be dead," Robyn said.

"I'll be right back." Spear glared, scraping her chair back.

When she was gone, I turned to Robyn and said, "Sounds mad, doesn't she?" Then I gave Robyn my all-out smile. Dimples included. "Pretty brave leap on the train. I knew you'd make it."

"I told you I'd been a gymnast," Robyn said. "What do you think Logan thought of his train ride? I didn't get a chance to ask him."

"Frightened to death probably."

"Poor Logan." Robyn closed her eyes a moment. "When we got here, all he wanted to do was go to sleep in his own bed."

"He held on to my neck with a stranglehold, and we just rode the rails. Got cold, though."

"I hope his mouth's not going to be sore from that tape. I feel so guilty."

"It came off pretty easy," I said.

Robyn shook her head. "All those people standing at the railroad crossing, waiting for the train to go by so they can cross the tracks and get down to the levee to board that gambling boat. They watched us jump from the train—"

"—hit the ground, tumble in the grass, and run like hell," I finished for her.

"They must've thought we were crazy."

"Did you hit Mud on the head with a Colt 45 bottle?"

"Right on the back of the head," Robyn said. "It shattered just like on TV." Robyn reached across her chair, gripped my hand, and circled an arm around my shoulder. "I can't thank you enough. Honest."

"It's not over," I said. "The cops have got to find those creeps."

"What happened to your pigtail?" she said, her eyebrows suddenly lifting. She felt the base of my neck.

"Um . . . I cut it off."

"When?"

"This morning. I should've done it a long time ago."

I wanted to kiss Robyn right there in the police station, even with all the cops bustling about. No law against kissing in the police station, was there?

But suddenly Sergeant Spear appeared, standing behind her desk. Looking pale.

"That was the hospital," she said. "Emergency room."

"Oh, my God! Logan . . . ?" Robyn's hand clamped her mouth for a second. "Tom and Elaine . . . ?"

My heart gave a panicky beat.

I was thinking what Robyn must have been thinking; Alan broke into Tom and Elaine's house. He was waiting for them. He'd hurt Logan! He'd hurt Tom and Elaine! Maybe he'd killed someone! Why hadn't the cops given them protection? *Jesus!*

Spear shook her head and sat down.

"Accident victim. We got a nine-one-one about an hour ago. Kid's friend called."

My spine tingled. I glanced at Robyn. She looked pale.

Spear said, "Our accident people didn't know there was a connection, though. They got to the scene, investigated, and left about the time I sent my people to the Standard Hotel."

"What happened?" Robyn said.

"This kid says he ran five blocks to find a pay phone and call nine-one-one. Then he ran back to his friend. Accident happened only a half block from the Standard Hotel."

"Alan Blythwood?" I said.

"No identification on him. Kid with a red heart that's dripping blood tattooed on his right wrist, though. According to the medical examiner."

I felt as if I'd been kicked in the stomach

"That's Alan . . ." Robyn's voice cracked, wavered.

"We got the one kid in custody," Spear said. "Calls himself Mud. Says his real name is Lester Simpson. He and his friend have been in town three weeks, living on the streets."

Somehow I managed to get air back into my lungs.

"Blythwood's been stalking Robyn and me," I said.

"His friend says the Blythwood kid tried to jump a freight train. He was chasing somebody. Couldn't hang on. Fell under the wheels."

I swallowed.

Trembling, Robyn closed her eyes and lowered her head into her hands. I nudged my chair closer to her, wrapped my arm round her shoulder, and kissed her on the forehead.

"Train severed his legs," Spear said. "Kid bled to death."

twenty-five

Two weeks later, on a Friday afternoon, after last period, Thompsonville Mayor Ben Cunningham was slated to address us high school students at the beginning of the pep assembly for the Thompsonville-Riverview football game. Our last home game. We were 6-1. Looking good. Ranked seventh in state polls.

Just before the assembly, Coach Maddox sent a message to me in geography class, asking me to stop by his office first.

When I arrived, he was sitting behind his desk, hands laced behind his head, smiling. You don't see that very often from him, not during the season anyway. Relaxed. Smiling. He pointed at the chair in front of his desk. "Sit down."

Books under my arms, I pulled out the chair and eased into it, wondering what was up, hoping this wouldn't take long because I wanted to get to the gym early so I could talk to Robyn a second before I sat with the team. She was going to interview the mayor for a story for the school newspaper. Her last assignment for the paper. Every second with her was precious.

Maddox said, "No time for bullshit here. What I want to tell you is I got a call this morning from a school interested in you. Guess who?"

I thought he must be kidding. I shrugged and said, "Sisters of Charity somewhere."

"Hell, no! Ellsworth, Iowa. That's not shabby, Stony. They've got a great junior college program going. They feed a lot of Division One schools like Iowa, Wisconsin, Minnesota."

I sat straight. "How did you do that?"

"Friend of mine's an assistant there. I sent him a few game films."

"I can't believe it."

"They're interested in Brian, too. I've already talked to him. He's going to give it a shot. How about you?"

"Oh, wow! You bet."

"They'll be sending you letters. Someone will call you on the phone. Be ready."

"I will."

"You've got talent, Stony. You have no idea how much."

I rubbed the back of my neck. I still couldn't believe he did this. "Thanks," I said and felt humbled.

"Had to be honest, though," Maddox said. "Told Brewster you had damn poor grades your first three years of high school. But this year you've shaped up. Told them you had a chance at some As and Bs. Brought an F in American Lit up to a B-minus in the first quarter. You're working hard this year. Taking charge of your life. Fighting to keep yourself eligible. You can do even better. Am I right?"

"Maybe all As by the end of the semester," I said.

"Great. Stay focused. If we keep our season going and win the state championship, that'll be another feather in your cap."

"The whole team feels nothing's going to stop us."

"Got to take your SATs."

"This spring, Coach."

"You stay on track, Stony, people out there will take notice."

I glanced at my watch. The assembly was in five minutes. Two-thirty.

Coach Maddox cleared his throat. "Um . . . this girl you've been hanging with, this Robyn Knight, has been good for you."

"She's helped me a lot."

"That ordeal you two went through a couple of weeks ago has made both of you kind of famous around here. Heroes—big story about both of you in the Sunday paper."

"Neither of us wanted that."

"Thing is, she's in my PE class but—well . . . I signed her drop card today. I just wondered . . ."

"She's from Connecticut." I shrugged. "She's going home."

"That's too bad."

"Yeah." Now I looked at the wall clock. "Coach, I've got to go."

"Me, too."

But before he could rise from behind his desk, I jumped up and shook Coach Maddox's hand. "Thank you!" I said. "Thank you very much!"

• • •

I arrived at the gym too late to talk to Robyn. She was already seated on a folding chair behind the speaker's podium talking to the mayor, also seated. She was taking notes.

As the gym flooded with laughing, skylarking kids, I took my seat with my teammates in the bleachers right next to Brain.

I think maybe his grin was wider than mine.

"You talk to Maddox yet?" he said.

"Just a minute ago. Ellsworth wants both of us."

"Imagine," he said. "Two hicks from Hickory Ridge— Ridge rats."

"Will we kick ass or what!" I said, and we both slapped each other's palm with a resounding high-five.

I knew the mayor wanted to urge us on to victory tonight, but I also knew he wanted to commend high school students, teachers, and administrators for extending the HELP program into the elementary and junior high schools, which in this town were just across the street from the high school. The idea behind the program was to train high school students so that they could use a free period a day to help younger kids with their math, reading, spelling, and writing. Like Robyn had helped me.

I'd volunteered to be part of the HELP group. I would help elementary kids with reading and writing. Imagine that.

• • •

After the assembly, I waited in my truck in the school parking lot for Robyn. The October afternoon was sunny but cool with a bright blue sky.

It was Alicia who arrived before Robyn did, her smirking face suddenly appearing at my driver's side window. I hadn't talked to her since she'd told me about Mindy's running away with Eric Small.

I cranked my window down. "What's happening? Your eye looks good."

"Thought you'd like to know—Mindy called."

"Really?"

I felt my face turning into a frown.

Was Mindy coming back to school? Since Robyn would be gone, would she try to wiggle her way back into my life?

Could I handle that? Could I say no?

"She coming back to school?" I said.

"Not hardly." Alicia tilted her head. "She's pregnant. She's getting married. She wanted me to tell you."

I don't know if my frown turned to surprise or not—I really wasn't surprised. "Eric Small? It's his kid?"

"Naturally." Alicia stepped closer to my truck. "That's all she ever wanted, you know—to get married. To feel she belonged to someone. She doesn't even know who her dad is."

"I know that. I hope she'll be happy, honestly I do."

"Like I believe you."

"If you talk to her again, tell her what I said. I'm happy for her."

"She's more a woman than that bag of bones you're dating now."

"You don't know anything about Robyn Knight."

Alicia's upper lip curled. "No more blow jobs, I'll bet."

I wanted to reach through my open window and slap Alicia.

Instead, I smiled and said, "I like you, too, Alicia. Have a nice day." I cranked the window up and watched her stride away across the parking lot.

I'd meant what I'd said: I hoped Mindy would be happy.

• • •

A minute later, Robyn climbed into my truck and closed the door. She leaned over and kissed me. She wore blue jeans, a black turtleneck, and the gold-and-blue letter jacket I bought for her eighteenth birthday last week. I spent the forty-five dollars I owed her plus more but was damned glad to do it.

I felt no need to tell her about Mindy. Mindy, for sure, was no longer a factor in our lives.

"I'll give you a ride home," I said. "I tried to tell you before the assembly. But Maddox cornered me."

"Can't. I've got to go back to the pub office and write my story. The mayor wants to open the high school gym one night a week for kids."

"Think he can do it?"

"If the school board and city can come up with some funding."

"Guess what?" I said.

"What? What's the big smile for? Your dimples look a mile deep."

I grabbed her hands.

I explained Ellsworth Junior College was interested in both Brian and me to play football. "Can you believe it?"

"Oh, Stony," she cried, and flung her arms around me. Hugged me. "Why not believe it? You're great."

"I don't know about that."

"You deserve it! Brian, too."

"All I know is we're damned happy."

She said, "It's more than playing football, though. You've got to decide what you might like to major in."

"Something to do with the wilderness," I said. "Like lakes, rivers, and streams. A game warden maybe."

"An environmentalist?"

"That's it. Someone who protects water resources."

"Are you listening to yourself?"

"What?"

"You're making plans for your future."

"And what are you going to be?"

I'd asked her that before. She'd said she was undecided between journalism or psychology. Now she said, "I think I'd like to head up a shelter for battered women. Maybe write a newsletter."

"That would be helping people and making a difference for sure."

"Absolutely."

I leaned over and kissed her again.

"I'll see you and Logan after the game tonight?" I asked.

"Right."

Tom, Elaine, Logan, and Robyn went to last Friday night's game. My mom and dad, too. Both sober. They all met and liked each other.

During the game, I played tough. Eleven tackles, two sacks, a recovered fumble. We won 28-3.

"And you're coming over after?" Robyn said.

I nodded. "I won't stay late. I promise."

"That's all right. I can nap on the plane. If Logan does."

I bit my bottom lip. Looked out my window at the kids lighting up cigarettes as soon as they were ten feet from the school building. Guys kissing their girlfriends between parked cars and trucks. I watched other cars and trucks lurching, screeching, racing out of the parking lot.

Robyn was leaving tomorrow.

Eight o'clock.

Logan and Robyn flying away.

Despite my happiness about Ellsworth, the thought of Logan and Robyn leaving was a knife plunged into my heart. Now that Alan Blythwood could no longer harm their daughter and grandson, her folks wanted them home.

I understood their reasoning.

Understood Logan's and Robyn's happiness.

But their leaving was killing me, though I tried to hide it.

Robyn looked at her watch. "I have to get going."

I hoped my eyes weren't suddenly glassy. "I'm going to miss you when you're gone. We hardly had a chance."

"You'll be busy keeping your grades up. Getting ready for your SATs. Working with HELP."

"That's not being with you."

She squeezed my hand. "We have tonight, Stony."

She had promised to visit next summer and to find a job here so she and Logan could stay, and we could be together before heading off to college.

Would she really return? For a Ridge Hick? Maybe she would. I'd have to wait and see.

She kissed me again. "Tonight, Stony."

"Tonight."

Just being with her was magic. Listening to her. Holding her. Kissing her.

"See you," she said. "Good luck."

"Thanks."

She slid out of the truck, closed the door, and I watched as she marched toward the school. I loved this girl.

I started my truck and headed home.

Mom would have an early supper ready for me.

We had been eating all our suppers together now, Dad bypassing Foggy's, coming right home—I'm not kidding. That started two weeks ago when Mom hired Vernon Purdy to help run the bait shop in the afternoons and evenings so maybe she wouldn't have to close it for good and could be home and do what she wanted and, of course, keep better track of Dad.

Working on weekends, Dad and I had half the house painted.

I hoped all this family togetherness lasted, especially the part about Dad's staying out of Foggy's. But I was afraid to be too optimistic.

As with Robyn's promise to return to Thompsonville next summer, I'd have to wait and see.

twenty-six

Robyn was snuggled deep into my arms on the couch in the den of Tom and Elaine's house. They were in bed sleeping. Logan was in bed sleeping. I'd heard the grandfather clock strike in the living room. *Boing.* One AM.

"It's all right, if you want to," Robyn said, quivering a little in the shadowy light from a lamp lit in the corner.

A lump formed in my throat, and I didn't answer.

"I'm not scared," she said. She touched my cheek with her fingertips. Her scent was so delicate but intoxicating, it made me a little dizzy. "I'm telling you fear's not an issue anymore. Okay?"

"Okay."

Everything had been perfect so far. We won our game 35-21. I had another great night. Tom, Elaine, Logan, Robyn, my mom and dad—everyone saw the game. Robyn and I went out by ourselves after. Skipped the Romp in the Woods. Ate Mexican. Laughed a lot.

Perfect so far.

But I didn't want to destroy anything with Robyn like I had with Mindy, so these past weeks I had learned to be content with simply holding Robyn in the dark and kissing her. Hands at home.

And now she was telling me it was okay. So naturally, my hand was thinking of creeping under her blouse. Or maybe into her jeans.

Damned if I do, damned if I don't.

She said, "Maybe you're the one who's scared."

I tried to swallow the lump in my throat.

Did she think I was the stud Mindy described on the girls' restroom at school? I wasn't.

I kissed Robyn's eyelids, nose, cheeks.

I stayed away from her lips. They would surely toss me over the edge. I mean, I didn't want us to be like lots of other couples—settling for a one-night stand, never speaking again.

I kissed her neck, my lips working their way around her dangling earrings, which played with my nose.

"I might never see you again," I said, "and I'm afraid I might ruin us with one wrong move."

She pulled back, and I felt her staring at me in the darkness. "You're wonderfully thoughtful." Her breath was raspy. "Anyone ever tell you that?"

A warmth invaded my face.

"Not lately," I said, and felt my hand itching for action. "Not any running backs, anyway."

"Stony, listen to me," she said. She cupped my face in her palms. "No matter what happens right now, I'll be back next summer."

"You promise?"

"Logan and I. And we'll see what happens then. Nothing has to happen now, if we don't want it to. All right?"

"You'll be back?"

"From now till June is not such a long time. We can write. Talk on the phone. You should get a computer—"

"I'm going to do that."

"—and we'll email each other. Explore our relationship."

I gave a little nod. "We've got to be smart about this."

"I haven't always been smart. Haven't always made wise choices."

"I'm trying to," I said. Then, "But you will be back?"

"Count on it. No matter what happens now."

She kissed me, then buried her face in my neck once more, her hair a whiff of flowers.

My hand relaxed. Decided to be cool.

I drew in a big breath with my whole body, until I thought my lungs would explode. I let it out slowly through pursed lips, and Robyn snuggled herself again into my arms.

Discussion Questions for

derailed

1. Why do you think such a smart, talented girl like Robyn Knight would allow herself to be abused by her boyfriend?

2. Explain what major events in the story lead to Stony's change in attitude about his future.

3. Explain how the final chapter supports the story's overall theme.

4. What do you think the future holds for Robyn and Stony?

5. In what way will the story's events affect Stony's and Robyn's futures?

6. How would you explain the relationship between Stony and Mindy Hillman? Was this true love?

7. What do you think will happen to Mindy?

8. If you were Robyn or Stony, how would this experience affect your life?

9. The young adult characters in this story seem to be making, or have made, wrong choices for themselves. In each scenario, what would have been a better choice?

10. How do you think all of this affected Logan?

11. What do you think the title means? What does it mean to be derailed?